THE GHOST OF UNDERSTANDING

The Ghost Of Understanding

A NOVEL

JEAN SMITH

ARSENAL PULP PRESS
Vancouver

THE GHOST OF UNDERSTANDING
Copyright © 1998 Jean Smith

ARSENAL PULP PRESS
103-1014 Homer Street
Vancouver, B.C.
Canada V6B 2W9

The publisher gratefully acknowledges the support of the Canada Council for the Arts for its publishing program, and the support of the Book Publishing Industry Development Program and the B.C. Arts Council.

Typeset by the Vancouver Desktop Publishing Centre
Printed and bound in Canada

CANADIAN CATALOGUING IN PUBLICATION DATA:
Smith, Jean, 1959-
   The ghost of understanding

   ISBN 1-55152-050-8

   I. Title.
PS8587.M544G56 1998   C813'.54   C98-910078-2
PR9199.3.S551565G56 1998

Thank you, Duane Crone, Peter Jefferies, David Lester, Dirk Hugsam, and Alan Twigg.

Foreshadowing Index

INTRODUCTION

Sound and light are linear systems. Light travels in straight beams penetrating the dark, it passes through itself and through sunlight. When I went alone, in silence, to travel through linearity, binary systems, and opposites, I was looking for methods of understanding that were outside duality. What I found was a self-sustaining system of energy creation that had provided water and power to a small community for hundreds of years.

I was working towards the edge of chaos, from solid to fluid, to what is hidden in what I think of as darkness. Somewhere between the freezing and thawing of water, between order and chaos, there is a relatively balanced place where the tension of these parameters creates and maintains transition. Transition. At what point does John Lydon turn into Johnny Rotten? It's too simple to say ego and alter ego. Sitting at the other end of a hockey arena about twenty years after someone called it punk, I tried to imagine Johnny's face. In my mind's eye I saw him at the height of the Sex Pistols' notoriety. The history of punk, the original reason and meaning for and of these songs, created a linear stamp on my thoughts. I wasn't aware of punk the first time around; I found out about the Sex Pistols long after they were finished. I saw PiL at Roseland in NYC in the spring of '81. They'd already been around a couple of years, the Sex Pistols were ancient history by then. The Sex Pistols in '96? I sat, immobilized, thinking: if they'd come back for the money—good for them.

If they'd come back to alter history again, to inform on history—better still. Some pragmatists wanted them to lie down in the pages of history with epitaphs they'd written themselves. It's disturbing for some people to be confronted by that which promised to be dead. It was always hard to look Rancid, The Offspring, and Green Day in the eye. Now it's impossible. Johnny Rotten is revered and emulated and that was never the point.

Did I tell you about the time we played at Rancid's warehouse in Oakland? We'd gone over our time. We were totally rushing through our set and were told by a Rancid member that we had to shut down—it wasn't a show that had anything to do with them, he just appeared from behind a closed door with this silly haircut. So Dave completely unplugs and keeps playing and I'm singing without a mic—like his amp is not connected to a power supply—and the Rancid guy comes out again to say we have to stop because his unamplified electric guitar is too loud!

(On the punk rocker's fear of punk rock.)

From the chaos of those original punk days, "order," by way of interpretation and imitation, has been defined and reduced so far that it's made punk mainstream. Now punk is a genre. Like rockabilly, it's a style. What happens next? When will order be disrupted by chaos and what will that place look like?

(After Slim's drum machine broke in NYC.*)*
SLIM: We started playing one song and as soon as it was over another song started and we just went with it and it happened again. So actually, it bodes well. We can play a number of our

songs—ones that we haven't been playing on the tour because they're too dire—but we're becoming a dire band.

JEAN: I like the sound of this. This machine has control over the band, over your mood, over your performance, over your capabilities.

SLIM: I know. The funny thing is, that's cool with us.

JEAN: You don't want to be responsible for your performance?

SLIM: Well, I can't be. We're the victims of whatever limitations we have and then we try to work within that framework. Even when it's an "all-organic" band, as they say, there is a set of limitations—what people can do, how much time we have to rehearse.

When the pendulum of social and political analysis swings up to the point where it changes direction, does it stop? Does the bow on a violin freeze for some fraction of time on the strings? I can't see the transition point, but that's what interests me. Not the transition of solid matter or motion, but ideas and their manifestation; a place where conviction and ambiguity meet. In a network of nerves and vessels, multiplicity is the spirit of knowledge and tolerance.

a) Plot Summary

The Ghost of Understanding doesn't pick up with Claudine where *I Can Hear Me Fine* left off. It illuminates another part of Claudine. *I Can Hear Me Fine* was a rapid-fire series of impressionistic sound-bytes that piled up in the form of dream, memory, vision, and flashback. Colour, sound, and a strange hyper-awareness of surroundings created a sensuous surreality.

Now Claudine reveals herself by inviting the reader into

her thoughts, to participate in a subliminally interactive text. This is a psychologically intimate document that reveals the diversity of her thinking. Claudine searches for the razor's edge between "order" and "chaos"—determined to find a comfortable way to exist. While acknowledging the two, she realizes she must explore darkness. Re-examining standard sexual fantasies places her outside the realm of rigid feminist analysis. Her willingness to participate in the realization/re-enactment of fantasy redefines power.

Even serious scientific exploration defies the linearity it professes to reveal. History is only one story. Language exists in time, but Claudine has an underlying demand to exist on different levels simultaneously. "Are we always drawing backwards?" asks Claudine of the mirror.

b) Plot Summary

Claudine's self-imposed exile and the simplicity of her rural lifestyle contribute to her compulsive chronicling of her thoughts, surroundings, the past, and a future she hopes to create from her experience. Her intellectual challenges are mirrored in the journey she takes to follow a system of aqueducts through the forest to their source. Along the way she reaches a satori-like state when she discovers the information needed to solve a great puzzle. The reader is invited into Claudine's thoughts to participate within a subliminally interactive text. "Are we always drawing backwards?" said Claudine to the mirror.

AMBITION

This begins in the dark. This darkness belongs to something we can't forget, even when we're asleep. It waits with us, seeping into our lives at an uneven, faltering pace, never far from where we think the surface is. It's always ready for us, to take our hands, to hold them motionless. And we don't even suspect it. We don't know it's there. Let me tell you about it, let me tell you how quickly it can rise up in you, in me. If you're driving fast at night and you decide to leave the highway the darkness is already ahead of you, around a corner you don't know you're going to take. How do I know? I've tested the darkness, I've spent time there, beside it, watching it. I'm almost ready.

The experiments have been different and I've never spoken to anyone about them. For all anyone else knows I'm living a normal life. An almost normal life. It's a matter of tension and control to find the designs. Within the rules of darkness I've melted glass back to sand, split yellow trees to splinters and wrung sap from the remains. It's a hurricane watch. I'm getting there.

I used to work days at the counter. He, sunken cheeks, paint flecks on his clothes, rubbed the dust from his hair and came to meet me. Together we drove home. My ambition faded. After that I used to work part time in an office. He built things that other people wanted. He couldn't keep them for himself. He always managed to pay half our bills. I began to move like him and picked up all his habits. He developed a fondness for rare wood from mainland China. Any extra time he had he spent sharpening his tools. My ambition slipped away, I couldn't stop the dullness from roaring in. Something was slowly rotting in my box of souvenirs. I took a token of my ambition and rolled it in my hands and like my plans, like my desire, it disappeared.

(On the matter of running a label and being in a band.)
JEAN: Last time I saw you you seemed pulled in two directions: label dude and artist guy.
SLIM: It's freakin' me out. It's freakin' my shit, man.
JEAN: Is it better to be out on the road?
SLIM: I feel so far removed from being a creative person, or even just being myself, instead of this automaton that performs for everyone else. I'm not being particularly creative on this tour, but I feel like it's a positive step because at least I'm being me and my sense of humour is coming back.
JEAN: See, I always just think of you as regular old Slim.

Maybe I'm making it seem too complicated, maybe you call it something else. Waking up, not knowing where you are, not knowing whose breathing you're listening to. Have you ever tried to dig straight through to the other side of the world? Lost before I knew it. Listening to another world's future breathing in the dark. Who is behind you, breathing in the dark? Is fear an accelerated form of wondering? Do you call it panic?

History survives—an extinct creature, an antiquated word, an unrecognizable shape. We've mistaken its origin, but we know it's there. Somewhere in me, when people say, "The moon is sinking into the horizon," I believe it is. I am running with rabbit leggings, looking behind me as I pound against the crust of spring snow. A wolf runs after me, tongue lolling to one side. Cedar boughs whip against me and the full moon sinks into the lake, creating darkness. Hiding. A chance.

These spells are my imagination and they occur when I'm on the verge of relaxing, between tension and relaxation.

I am taking a tuna sandwich out of plastic wrap on the first spring day warm enough to eat outside. Office workers are sitting on the cement edges of the fountain, they push back hair in the breeze, look for sunglasses in purses, drop shoes to wriggle toes.

I am sitting alone, enjoying the mutual happiness of a season turning, warming up. I am feeling outside of things, but somehow unconditionally connected; my imagination goes. I am in the middle of the city, following the person ahead of me and suddenly I become a witness and yet I can't recount the facts of the accident. I know it involved a pedestrian and a car. I was at once part of connection and disorientation. I was skinning a small animal with a crooked knife, my hands flicking the entrails, separating the flesh from the fur. Deep in the forest, two hundred, three hundred, five hundred years ago.

(In the beginning.)
SLIM: Starting at the beginning. . . . Were the original methods used by Mecca Normal out of necessity or ideal?
JEAN: Slim, it was neither. It was a total lack of knowledge, understanding, and scope that led Mecca Normal to any method. Then it became, simultaneously, necessity and ideal. It's easier to stand by a band whose formation you invented. If you follow the rule book and someone tells you you're wrong, then where do you stand? I think things have changed

for bands wanting to put their own records out—the information is out there.

SLIM: It is for urban bands, but we still get a lot of bands outside cities asking us to put out their records and we write back and tell them how to do it themselves.

JEAN: When we put out our first album there were some people in Cleveland who contacted us and asked for some of our records. Pollution Control. They sent out packages to radio stations—a bunch of records they liked that probably never would have got around otherwise. Then we started getting letters and playlists from places like Moscow, Idaho. We realized we could make contact with people.

December '91

   Hi! It's enough! I'm Dirk and I like your musik. After one year looking for your records I'm tired of not finding it. I'm interested in all your stuff. Every record, tape; oh yes for t-shirts or tour posters too. If you can send me anything, it would be very nice.

   In this letter I send you 100$ and this heavy duty cigarettes and if there is any money left use it up for a beer and enjoy and maybe you get a kick for another great song.

   If you will ever get to Germany let me know, maybe I could be helpful with some tour contacts.

   So this was my idea.

Dirk

April '92
Hello Jean,

   Thank you for all the records and for the t-shirt too. The packet took a long time, maybe it went by submarine across the north pole, but I'm not sure. Thank you for your booklet of poetry. You're right,

16

*my English understanding isn't so easy, but I am together with time
and a good dictionary so I can understand your lyrics and I like this
kind of writing and singing.*

*So I talked to a few promoters about a tour, but it wasn't so
promising (crazy guys!). OK. Now my idea. I will do it for you!*

*Normally I make some concerts here in town, sure, not a whole
tour, but why not? I know most of the special clubs which are important
for you and I know a lot of people. I think it works!*

Please consider this and if you want to do it, so tell me.

*And tell me what are your conditions? How long you like to
go on tour? How many gigs you'd like to play and when. For the
equipment and things like that too. Oh and don't forget if you like to
smoke another package of the cigarettes tell me.*
Dirk

The rocks on the beach are warm colours; warm greys, warm
browns. Dull, rubbed smooth by the tides. I am lying face
down on the rocks, pushing my fingers through them. My eyes
are closed, I can smell the salt. The rocks are small, they fit in
my hands. I've stopped waiting. Tension disappears down-
ward. The side of my face is pressed against the rocks. I am
only the translator here and I'm still not convinced I understand the language, but the process surrounds me whether I
understand it or not. You'll have to accept my work as interpretation. Next, you become the translator, involved prior to
recognizing multiplicity. The darkness seems to demand an
endless shifting, a dense shuffling. The destruction of codes.

I remember that girl, alone on a beach, fending off
desperation, filling notebooks with a silent scream. In the
transition from a daughter to a wife I made a list that read like
errands to be run. The list was intended to define the future

on paper. I got tired of recipes and redecorating rooms. Inch by inch, but not without asking, I pulled away. Nowadays I don't want to own a horse. I don't need to see Paris in April.

The rocks are cold fingers; magnets restructuring molecules into new patterns. Constant motion. There is never repetition. The sea is breathing in my ears, a conductor of sound. Whose future am I listening to now?

Crimson drops the levels, casting molten iron to the sea. Underwater near the ruins of the shipyard, time is slow and energy is speed. Waxy laughter breaks across the back of history. Fingers pinching dust in black caverns, searching for a method that exists in a void. Rifling through history, investing in past lives, the honeycomb of doubt crumbles at the slightest touch.

Every day at about four the crows fly east. Their course changes with the seasons. The crows fly back from the sun like an answer. I'm not sure if it's an answer to a question or a problem. The directions are half-written disappointments. Some things can be left without solution. The sun smells sweet without compulsion.

The slow days will take us together. I'll pay you what I want to owe you. I expect you to give me what I want.

Sick of land faith on a mile. Sick of gravity's sheen Sunday at noon, believing we can't fly. Sheer pink in a thousand summers' eyes, frayed edges. Some things can be left without solution.

Snow traces a white outline on the trees. A book open on the windowsill, open to the pages with a drawing of bodies falling through history, searching for the light to separate them from the dark. The book is so small compared to the original drawing. Taking it in with one glance, as if it was just a thought, a gesture, it's easy to forget that the bodies fell with such weight and power. If you choose the misconception as a reference, as a guide to understanding, you will reproduce nothing. Really nothing.

April '92
Dirk, hello,

I'm sorry it has taken me so long to write back. We have been talking about the tour idea. I hope you're still thinking about the booking idea. I've talked to a few people who have toured recently in Europe and they say good things. Basically we would hope to pay for our expenses. I would guess we could do about fifteen shows in three weeks, the last three weeks of October. I've booked many tours so we can figure it out together. I'll send you all the promo stuff you'll need: records, info, photos, articles. Let me know how much of what. Do you have an answer machine? What hours are good to talk to you? I have some more questions before we can commit ourselves. Putting all the time and energy, not to mention the cost, of doing a tour into someone we have not even met is a difficult thing to do. The more specific information we can get the easier it will be to make the best arrangements. We need to know your recommendations on transportation. Do we rent a car? Will you be able to come with us? What would the distances between shows be like? We would like to do everything as cheap as possible. Is it possible to stay with people rather than go to hotels? The one requirement we have is that the tour pays for itself. We would like to have a pretty relaxed time too. We like to have a lot of fun on tour and not be too tired. Our idea of fun is a bit of sight-seeing, eating, and hanging out with people. We don't have to headline, we'd like as many people as possible to see us. Please fax me your phone number. Bye for now!

Jean

May '92
Dear Jean,

Let's dare it! As both of us don't know each other I hope on good working together too. So I try to give you as precise information as possible now. My first problem. I already announced you coming and fixed some dates for the first three weeks of October. Is it OK for you to accept this time? Please tell me quick. Next thing. Touring with a car that you rent from North America would be best. What kind of car? I think you know best how much space you need. As far as possible I will join you. Important. Tell me what additional equipment I have to organize. Expect a distance of 200-300 KM between shows. It is usual that the venues organize accommodation.

I'll try my best to check out good places good people to make a good and relaxed tour with a lot of fun. The only problem could be our communication because my English isn't too good, but I think we can handle that. I prefer writing to telephoning, but this is my number. . . . Take it easy and have patience with my English, OK?

So far so good, till next time,
Dirk

If you live your life examining misrepresentations you might never notice where the inconsistencies are, the imperfections that allow breathing. This is the darkness you won't see. If you are determined to imagine that there are no errors in other people's examinations, then you will be bolted to stillness. Forced to stand alongside the unrelenting pulse beats of light and dark, you will have dulled what could have been. Where do these accidents occur?

When I told Max I was seeing another man he said he'd like to wait before he talked about it, before he could talk about it. Then he wrote me a letter. Just as well I wasn't home when he came and left it inside on the table, written on my paper with my pen.

Dear Claudine,

I came here to tell you what I've told you before. You thought you could pass my hand, but I found a way to the back of your mind and I took it. I struck something in you. I came here to tell you I've seen this before. I did not want to have this happen again.

You weren't here so I invited myself in. You tried to dismiss me, you told me I was wrong and that you had always realized that I wasn't the one for you. I've had this happen before. I walked in the dark, up to the house, and knocked. I came to tell you I've seized your mind and you'll never know peace in your heart again because you're mine. Now you're mine.

Always, Max

He sounded mad, perhaps he was drunk and mad. Normally he was a pretty good writer. I wondered what form he thought the seizure of my mind would take. I laughed about it at the strangest times; chopping wood, clipping my toenails, spreading peanut butter on toast.

His next letter arrived. He'd addressed it to me and sent it to Ray. The return address was on the other side of the country. He'd gone home to his mother's again.

Dearest Claudine,

Around 9:30 in the morning. The radio is on, sun streaming through the window. It's a beautiful day. I've been going through my boxes and cases, seeing what's here, keeping stuff, throwing stuff away.

I feel sort of silly having left you that note. I think you probably guessed that I was a bit drunk. I should have tried to talk to you, but

21

a flight home came up for a really good fare and as you can see, I took it. I know I was away a lot when we were together. I guess I hadn't added it up to almost half of last year. I want you to be happy and cared for and you're right—we did have some problems! I'm glad you have a good friend like Ray.

Anyway, I just thought I'd let you know where I am and that I'm doing fine.

Take care,

Max

At first I thought he was brave, then I felt angry. I hadn't wanted to hurt him, but I guess I wanted him to ride in on a horse as big as two kingdom comes with a blade that, upright, would tower above us all; all three, blocking out the sun.

He'd handed me over willingly. Exquisite neutrality. What does my heart tell me? It must be a lot. I can't hear a single word, just the roar of blood swishing and baritone whispers blocking out beats and stresses of advice. I could only make out one line of indelible ink, a stamp of disapproval.

Simmering fidelity like it was a stew of too tough meat gives you a stringy tasteless dish that leaves you wanting, not more, but something better.

It's good to be at ground level again. For a while, at least, the clouds will stop pressing against my eyes, shrieking the question I've already answered.

I was the moon while he was either the earth or the sun on my back, larger than life. The orbit—mine or his? Around him or is it with me, that around we go? He'd miscalculated my strength. I'd hinted that I was weak. I am persuaded by strength and this time I've found and lost some of mine.

The day I was convinced it was over I'd filled out a form

and marked the "single" box with an X. Until then, I hadn't felt single for a long time. I'd tried to feel anything but and I'd won by giving myself to him. Going out alone at night with half the power missing means I look alone, without him to lean on, even though he never thought I leaned. He forgot that the eyes of spies were on my heart. I'd let my guard down. I know the rules. It was a reaction. I asked, "What's Ray doing to me?"

And Ray kept thinking, "For how long?"

"Are we always drawing backwards?" said the lady to the mirror.

What knife is turning? I can't feel him. Everything else, everything else except this not being able to feel him is a pounding just below where my heart used to be. Nothing was ever solved. There is a panel missing from a black-and-white cartoon strip. I wave him away, stare into the dark corners I had let him peer into, trying to find out what he knows about me. I can't think of anything sadder than admitting that this never really happened. What knife is turning in me? I'm the one who talks too much. He's self-contained. I always thought his motivation to know me was odd. He learned about me by listening, without telling me what he thought. Feel. I've been on a spree of overcompensation. He asks, or rather says rhetorically, "Can't you just sing the words off the page? You wrote them."

"Not if I don't like the song," I reply.

He doesn't talk much, he finds a place halfway that allows me enough room to continue, a maintenance level. If there is a problem we know it will be gone by morning. Never mentioned. What knife?

Where does he really live his life? What is he protecting? I can see the edges of the trap I built. I'm constricting my worth and from the trapper's view I watch me, he's beside me, we watch me squirm, belly up. I'm beyond his reach. Arms at his side, he watches. I lie in my own trap. He blinks and turns away.

I've let him leave me stranded when I know I'm fine alone. In this case he's disabled by the words that don't explain the why-oh-why? away. I'm carving out a calling after him, nothing as vast as nothing new. The terms remain the same. I can't be stranded when I want to be alone.

Was it love or endurance? In a normal day his gaze is cloudy, he looks distracted when I speak. He doesn't need to understand or be understood. I'm drowning in our mutual self-defeat, flinging down thoughts like cards.

"I call you and raise you. . . ."

The thing that was supposed to mean something took a long time to make. I suspect it was incomplete, filed along with all the secret languages that avoid saying what is felt. His words sidestep his own organization, a hypothesis on splayed, burnt matchstick legs staggering into a topiary maze, into anti-language. He can make the right sounds to show how hard he tried. He states his case, a shimmering mirage to lope after, unattached to situations and evidence. He takes what isn't freely given, leads a life without seduction, washing his hands of any obligation to explain himself, his exorcism is an imitation and I suspect that's what leaves me cold.

DEPARTING

You've phoned in your departing flight back to where you came from. You've started calling it home. I can barely feel these endings any more. You're always saying you have to leave. I'm the one who battles us back, keeping us together. Now there are no more plans for which I have to sharpen my skills, walk on burning glass, to make some dream come true. You're still wandering around town smoking, wearing the coat I bought to sell but gave to you when the weather got cold.

I can't understand the motives anymore. Our lack of interest in each other sexually keeps us demoralized and distant. Is there no time to fix the damage? Sex is the last problem I thought we'd have to deal with. I used to think it was great that I fantasized about you, about us, when we were apart. Fantasy returns to where it belongs—the imagination. The men there are meatier than you, their long curly hair falls over my face, they hold me around my waist and pull me close. When they come in my mouth they say it feels like electricity down their legs. They fuck me until it's light out, I wash down their cum with champagne and laugh. A lot. These men look at me when I take off my clothes—you turn away.

You say you just don't have the life-skills to make it here. I know standing outside a liquor store with a guitar isn't much of an idea, but you want to go home, live at your mom's house, and collect welfare—as if that's a plan. You think I should give up this place and go with you. Well, I've met your mom and seen her house and it's really cool that she smokes

25

pot and swears, but I don't want to trade one stupid town for another. I think living with your mom, collecting welfare, and then coming back in the spring, is a stupid plan. I know you said you'll send me what you can to cover the rent, but I don't really want your welfare money. I kind of like being off welfare.

I've been through this before. One of these days I'm going to call you by the wrong name: Bruce. Bruce said he couldn't stay, he said it again and again. I panicked and started wrecking everything between us. I finally got some friends to take him out of our apartment. I took all his stuff down to the Greyhound station, put it in lockers, and mailed him the keys. He's still here—three years later. It was just about this time of year too. Funny how things repeat themselves. Same thing. I couldn't cover for him, I can't cover for you. I've figured out how to get by, but just barely.

You're evaporating our future with your frequent flyer points. I told you I'd give you some of mine, but you're hooked. You have to fly home to get a free flight back. Except that you won't have anything to come back to. I could have accepted a visit, but then you said you'd send money every month. How many months are we talking about?

I'm not shattered. I'm too old for that. I'm practical. Guys still look at me, but the fuck-you look I've employed to keep them at a distance is hard to drop and it's working a little too effectively lately. I'm no catch and men are quick to let me know it.

Last night I sat at my desk watching the sun go down. I was on the phone listening to Telepersonals; casual encounters, thirty to thirty-five. I'd recorded my temporary greeting, berating people for being shallow. That got me zero responses from the twenty males on the system. I changed my message, softening it. I described the sunset, said there was a hawk sitting on a telephone pole outside my window and asked if anyone else had noticed that the city's crow population flies east at this time of day. I got a very abrupt response from an impatient male voice: "What do you want off this line, anyway?"

I felt excluded from the exchanging of stats and preferences. I had not said that I was gorgeous, loved roller-blading and going to the movies. My next greeting announced that I was strutting around my penthouse apartment in black stockings sipping champagne, wondering who I'd be spreading my long legs for that evening. My line was clogged with Matthews, Mikes, and Pauls—all considered attractive and well-endowed. All wanting to relieve me of my loneliness, admonishing me for being alone, depriving them of me. Men have a way of trying to get what they want by correcting women. It is not something I find seductive.

In a dream I am standing with my arms casually above my head. Plain happiness, no self-consciousness, no awkward, useless anger or guilt. In the dream I am empty of criticism and judgement. I am laughing. I am content.

Battling across a country, a table in a bar, a bed, through thin air at high altitudes—too dizzy to remember all the details. Old soul, born old. I find sad men without anything to live up to and they seem to want forgiveness. They want to be the antithesis of a man. They want to be weak, without the ability to survive or make anything other than a sandwich for dinner. Why don't they re-invent the vehicle?

I am so free my wings ache from flying. I am almost free of myself. After last weekend I'm sure it's over. On the ferry back from the island I laughed as I read the personals in a publication that had systematically processed the poetry and personality out of every ad. An inordinate number of men liked building models from kits, collecting hockey cards, and "sports." Women claimed to be caring, honest and to enjoy crafts. I laughed, but I wondered what SWM, 34, 5'8", 140 lbs., quiet, attractive, mature, great smile, was like. You sat biting your nails. I rubbed my sore knee. Sore from falling into the jacuzzi at the hotel in Parksville. The trip was supposed to be sex-filled, restoring us, repairing the damage, but with my gouged-up knee and your bad back, nothing happened. I slammed doors, you went to bed early and got up late.

It feels like it's over, but you haven't left yet. You can't get a flight on the right airline for a month. Your mom sent you a hundred bucks in her Christmas card; a strange card claiming, "The one thing I'll always treasure is the memory of all the fun we've had being friends." It was addressed to both of us, but since I've only met her once I don't think her warm, treasured memories include me.

You're on the phone updating earlier departures due to cancellations. I'm waiting for you to get off the phone so I can call Telepersonals. You're scribbling down details, shifting the phone quickly to your other ear; it's sounding good. "Yes, yes, yes!" you answer excitedly.

I'm making notes of my own.

"Hi, this is Debbie, I have icicles hanging from my nipples, pink candy floss for hair. My ass is so big I can't fit in the seats at the movies. I'm looking for a man who doesn't have any frequent flyer points. Unemployed smokers, social drinkers, and nail-biters welcome."

From a sun-bleached chair with missing rungs on a porch of weathered boards, a book is dropped on its broken spine and a rigid man walks inside. The pages arch up, turning, the paper is torn and grey and he still doesn't know what it means. He lives in a strange desolation, stopped by a thought, caught in time. He has decided the book has the answer and its extraction is long overdue. He returns to the porch. He sits down in the chair and starts again with his obsession. His fingertips are smooth from his ritual turning. He is humiliated by a failure to learn. The method outlasting the tool. Every day he thinks about stopping, but he can't.

There is a belief in the perfection of information. It exists because it is exclusively unchallenged. I am a witness. Half hostage, half victim. Blackmail shifts around. There is a closing up and a drawing in. The spectacle is the reward. In a catalytic cycle, the universe behaves. A crowd chants out at ringside, calling for the revival of cruelty. Calling out for more. When a direction is taken it starts justifying itself, beginning by imposing a dismissal of all that's unexplored. Direction becomes a window in the semi-dark of night. We are peering in, or we are gazing out. And the crowd calls out for more, calling for the revival of cruelty.

(Jean Smith interviews K Records' Calvin Johnson on the phone.)
CALVIN: If you were some jazz loser and you were making up your song as you went along they'd call it improv and laud you for it, but otherwise you're faking it or something. I'm not sure where that comes from exactly.
JEAN: I think it's a view that actually prevents people from trying something themselves. They believe there has to be so much skill and God-given talent and crafting. The idea that somebody can just stand up and do something through the experiences they've had or the way they think—that's too

much for some people. It makes them feel like they're failing. If the essence is really that close to the surface and they can't tap into it, maybe it's easier for them to believe that it is fraud to do it, because if it isn't, that would mean they should be able to do it too, hence, they might be failing on a daily basis.

CALVIN: Or the fact that there are other people who have convinced them to believe all that is necessary, maybe those are the people calling it fraud.

JEAN: Totally.

CALVIN: So maybe if they believed what you were doing was legitimate they'd be admitting to this other fraud. If you were a man, people would look at it as cool that you could make things up off the top of your head, but when you're a woman doing it, it's somehow not legitimate. I see that those attitudes are still really prevalent and that's just one aspect of the social issue of women being involved in our culture, actively involved and recognized for it.

May 25, '92
Dirk,

OK, let's dare it! The first three weeks of October. We will be ready to start shows October 1. OK? Let us know. We will arrive in and leave from Frankfurt. I will pick up and return the car there. It will be a Ford Fiesta. I can get a good deal if I book it from a travel agent here. Do you drive? How old are you? Sometimes there is a different insurance rate for under a certain age. How long do you think we'd have to play for? Is it usually one or two sets? David will need to borrow a guitar amp. For the PA we need one vocal mic and one mic for the guitar amp. David doesn't want to plug straight into the board. I hope we don't have to pay extra for a soundperson. If there isn't a soundperson perhaps you could do it. We need monitors (fold back) as well.

What is your favourite and most delicious national meal? What is the weather like in October? Will everyone be drunk all month at Octoberfest? Have you been to North America? Do you have a job?

Jean

Hello Jean,

Thank you for your last fax. It was really nice and funny. I never was in North America but I stood half a day in Vancouver only at the airport. How old am I? Oh I'm just sixteen and I got my driving licence last week. I can do anything at all! Ahh not really! I am thirty-two years old and stand with both feets on the floor. I hope so, or where else? I can't give a whole curriculum vitae, not in a letter. Maybe when we meet us. At the moment I have no job. I did a regular job the last eight years. What's my favourite meal? Impossible to say because I am very thorny. But I like noodles. And you? Octoberfest! That's good! Because I live only ninety KM away Munich. But this party is too much for me. In my whole life I stayed only ten minutes and it was enough. Like a drunken Disneyland in leather pants. It's enough. Back to the tour. Usually the clubs have their own soundman, but if it's necessary I can try to do sound for you. I will organize an amplifier for David. If any special wishes tell me in time. I got English lesson from the library two month ago! Normally the clubs open 8-9, the bands start at 9:30-10 and play 1-1 1/2 hours.

What idea have you about pure holiday? If you want you can come down here and spend some days here in Bavaria. I could show you around.

OK?

Dirk

Evidently, Francisco Pizarro went from Spain to Peru in 1534. There, he had a salad of potato, wurst, and oranges, which he introduced to Europe upon his return. Facts are patternless, adrift, until we place them within the confines of concept. It seems like we'll do anything before we are ready to simply realize darkness. We prefer the light, a history, the ease of rivers flowing one way, stars reappearing in recognizable designs, charted waters. We are after rhythms, drawn to the most basic constructs of understanding.

Packed tightly around the roots of trees hundreds of years old, we will not claw away the density of our mistakes. Seeing the forest floor as a balance between interior and exterior puts us on our hands and knees, sifting through a partial explanation. It's what we can't see, can't name, can't put into the box of fate that keeps me awake before sunrise.

Standing up on the beach the wind pushes me, I sway, turn the collar of my housecoat up and walk towards the forest. In the places where moonlight hits twigs and frozen berries, the frost shines silver. The rest of the world is static in shadow. My hands are in my pockets. Periodically I stop walking to listen to the near silence. Looking back at the beach through the trees, the rocks are a homogenous blur. All variation and detail is lost at this distance. Beyond the beach the water is flat grey with white streaks travelling towards me. I walk farther into the forest, back towards the house. The sound of the sea changes the deeper I go, bouncing back off the cliff where water trickles through moss and ferns; shining, slippery, and dense. The stone house blends in. It is completely covered in moss, the glass in the windows shines like wet rock. My footsteps echo on wooden stairs. I hang onto the rail—I've slipped on these stairs too many times. The house is surrounded by poplars sucking up water from the ceaseless runoff. Winter is the only time the light penetrates the forest enough to touch the house. The leaves came off the poplars in only a few days this year, clattering through the branches, letting in the sun and moonlight.

I wipe my feet and as I'm opening the door I hear the kettle screeching on the stove, filling the cold room with steam. I'd forgotten I'd only gone outside to wait for the water to boil. The sea attracts me. When I'm in front of it, I'm mesmerized. To me, it's the largest expanse of darkness with the greatest surface area. A surface that challenges me to understand the obvious.

At my house death brings light. The new growth of spring is what brings the darkness here, sheltering the house from light, smothering it in pulses of shadow. The leaves propel themselves on their stems; futile fanning in the wind. For now, though, in winter, the trees are stiff in the cold of full exposure. Savouring the wait.

The house was built to conform to the side of the cliff. The cliff is actually the back wall. Water runs down it, ferns and ivy spread out from it into the main room. A trough at the base of the wall takes the water outside and into the creek to the sea. Only in the driest part of summer can I hear the sea. The water almost stops trickling and is overshadowed by a constant roar. The individual waves are too hard to separate audibly.

I re-mortared between the stones of the walls when I first got here, but I've tried to leave most of the place the way I found it. The windows don't really fit and the roof leaks. If I close one eye the flowers I painted on the inside walls are just colour, holding a purple glow. Sometimes I sit on the hard-packed dirt floor with my arms around my knees experiment-ing with focus, colour, and sound. I guess I daydream, matching colours with sound. Out of focus. The paintings are on long sheets of paper taped together and tacked near the ceiling. Watercolour flowers are outlined in black; huge bunches of flowers held by hands reaching in from the sides of the room. Old hands with misshapen, crooked fingers and blue fingernails. The paper is brittle and wrinkled. The paint ran until it hit the creases, then it followed those paths in all directions. The wall looks like stained glass, braided rivers intersect the ginger-pinks and reds of the flowers.

I built a shed made from the glass that I brought up from the beach. It's quite different from the house. It's waterproof and light. I found panes of thick green glass along the high tide line strapped between panels of bashed styrofoam. When I unlashed one I found that sand had worked its way in and had rubbed the glass to an opaque roughness. Glacial. I got the glass up to the house and leaned the panes together like a house of cards. Sumac trees formed the corners of the structure. I filled in the spaces with branches and a mixture of mortar and pebbles. When I wiped away the excess mortar I realized how beautiful the little rocks were all pressed together, finding the tightest way to fit. When the mortar was dry I lacquered the rocks, giving them the shine they had on the wet incline of the beach. I built my bed on the same incline as the beach. At night I imagine I'm on the beach, small rocks spreading out around my form. The rocks hold the heat of the day. I try to imagine that the warmth of my bed at night, eyes closed, is the warmth that the rocks collect all day, saved for the contrast of darkness.

I made all the furniture in the house out of bent wood. I cut thin branches from the poplars, ran a knife down them to take off the papery bark and any twigs, and then boiled them in the bathtub until they were supple enough to bend. The tub is outside. Water runs into it from a flume on the cliffside. I get a good fire going under the cast-iron tub and put it out when the water is hot enough for a bath. When I was making the furniture I kept stoking the fire and increasing the tension on the bent branches. I had twenty curves; some wide, others tight. I made two chairs, the table, and the bed by lashing the curves to framework that supported horizontal surfaces. In the hard edges of the stone room the curves in the furniture create a balance by contrast.

When I need something I seem to be able to find it or make it. I think I've almost always been this way. I figure out how to do things by looking around, thinking about how to utilize what's already there. I used to be the kid in the neighbourhood who fixed transistor radios and aquarium pumps. When I got older and started living alone I accumulated the usual number of objects and replaced them at regular intervals, but when I became more confident in the way I worked best, I was able to start on a course that deepened my ingenuity just by using it. In the end I was able to take a file and a piece of metal and work with the file until I had created a file with the file. After that it seemed normal to do so. Of course something is lost, but it's the kind of thing that can be watched to be remembered. You don't have to live within those restraints.

(On three of everything and Luther Perkins.)
SLIM: We're heading to Richmond, to Big Al's. He's got three of everything.
JEAN: You have to say it like that?
SLIM: Big Al has three of everything and he sells it cheap and he likes to deal.

JEAN: What are we talking about here?

SLIM: Three of everything. You want a weed whacker? He's got three of them. You want a motorcycle? He's got three of them.

JEAN: You're playing this place?

SLIM: We're going. . . . We're looking to buy. I'm in the market for a new guitar.

JEAN: "Looking to buy." What guitar-playing guy isn't?

SLIM: Well, I'm not a guitar-playing guy, but I just read about Luther Perkins. . . . You know who that is?

JEAN: Bet it's some old blues guy. . . . Oh, Carl Perkins' brother, from *Mutual of Omaha's Wild Kingdom*!

SLIM: No, it's actually . . . he played guitar for Johnny Cash. He was a shop owner until he was 28 years old and Johnny Cash's next door neighbour and best friend. Johnny Cash was like, "Hey, I want you to play guitar for me." So he never even picked up the instrument 'til he was 28 and he was a great guitar player. So that encourages me.

JEAN: But you don't have a Johnny Cash pestering you.

SLIM: Well, that's me.

I reject purity in favour of ambiguity. Maybe it's the easiest thing to do after you reject morality. I'm suspicious of ambiguity as an option, but it's what I'm thinking about now. How can I accept anything rigid after concluding that the patterns of pressure that we force on ourselves are delusions? Is it only a new mirage that I've fallen into?

In my mind I follow the path through the forest to the sea. Under the waves, in the motion of darkness, I test my vision. An astronaut. Waiting to dismiss anything as valueless. I have to.

Longevity starburst. Anti-design. Fish without arms fly

around the room, coaxing imposters to call the Rival Theories Hotline to mainline a dose of duality. Caving in. Passengers, scientists of fear, lean over the rail of the Titanic II, imagining the ocean floor. Caving in.

I surface and float on my back. Salt stings my lips and burns in my open eyes. There are many ways of doing things. I haven't figured out the clouds yet. I'm piecing things together, making things difficult, making what I need from nothing. Fortunately I don't want to duplicate the conveniences that allow a person to be pressed, a dry flat shape, into oblivion. I'm trying to be comfortable with hypocrisy and self-indulgence. I'm trying to avoid guilt and obligation. I rely on the darkness. I find what I need.

In Bavaria, Julia, Dirk's girlfriend, handed her apartment over to us. Usually evenings started across the street at Dirk's. Rainer, Dirk's brother, came over for dinner. Bubu showed up to finish off the leftovers. The usual thing to do after dinner was to go downstairs and around the corner to the Picadilly for a few beers. The place was great, it had a really good feel about it. They played great music: Barbara Manning, Pavement, The Clean, Superchunk. The beer was good and people made an effort to make conversations interesting. People were gracious. It felt very strange to be there, I was somehow not prepared. I am strongly based in language, especially as a singer. It was unnerving to have to put so much thought into getting ideas across. The younger people I met seemed to speak English amazingly well, but for people for whom school was long ago, the transition to English was more difficult. Dave and I got used to speaking in simple sentences at a slow speed, we did it when no one else was even around. That was strange. Most of the people we met wanted to speak English, so we didn't really learn much German. Dirk did an incredible job for us. He had a special idea about bringing a relatively, in fact, completely unknown band to Europe. The clubs were great, the money was amazing compared to North America. He did all the driving, sold our records for us after the shows, handled the money, and was a really good friend to us. He even laughed at our jokes.

JEAN: You know, when I think of K I don't think of an interest in overtly politicized dogma. I see you doing things that follow some of those sentiments, but the word from K isn't put together in a literal way. It's interesting that you were attracted to the Black Wedge because it was very literal.

CALVIN: One of my ideas, in the back of my mind, is that instead of saying that we're smashing sexism, we're trying hard not to be a macho rock 'n' roll label.

JEAN: Does it ever bug you how much Mecca Normal talks about things in literal terms?

CALVIN: No, I think it's great. For me the idea is we're trying to create an environment where those negative things don't exist. I think a lot of people who are making music in a political way . . . one criticism I might have is that they don't allow for dialogue. If you disagree with them they just turn off. I've encountered a lot of people who have strong political views who don't have a strong tolerance for other people's views.

JEAN: They need to get out more.

SHOE POLISH WING LATCH

It is dusk again. I sit down at the table and hold my steaming cup of tea with both hands. I used to hate the dampness, winter, and the dark. I am watching the light in the sky lose its brilliance, turning into warm yellow, dimmer and dimmer. I love this transition, I try to sit still and watch it every day. I hold the cup to my lips and the steam glistens in front of me, a spectrum of coloured particles. I feel energy returning, given back by the coming darkness. The floor and the wall are indistinguishable. I push the chair away from the table. The legs carve into the dirt, creasing the surface. I light the candles and the sharpness of the flames feeds back in the warped window glass, multiplying the pinpoints of light. I pull the sleek black curtains and the fabric catches on the roughness of my fingers. I pick up my half-smoked cigarette from the ashtray and light it. I stare at the tip, the ember. I tap the ash off and roll the end in the ashtray. I watch the steam from the tea mix with the smoke, passing through it like a crosswind, an ocean current. I pace slowly across the room, back and forth, scuffing the heels of my boots on the soft floor, listening to how they sound. I might never get used to it. I compare it to the sound of sidewalks and wood floors. I am haunted by the echoes of other surfaces. This place is so smooth. I swing open the stove door and smoke wafts into the room. I poke at the fire. I split another chunk of wood and fit it in the stove and feel the heat. I watch the burning shapes, the sizzling pockets of pitch. Sparks fly out and are extinguished immediately on the damp floor. The resurgence of heat starts the kettle whining, wavering low.

There are some things I've decided to forget about. Others slip away from me at dawn, never to be reclaimed. Or missed. They are gone, like the fading tip of an almost forgotten dream.

Clair and I pull into her long gravel driveway. The headlights flash on the gladioli, bent over from the heavy rain. At the end of the driveway, blocking us from getting into the garage, is a load of firewood. Clair shuts off the engine and we sit in the truck with the headlights on.

"There's more wood than I can use," says Clair.

"Where are you going to put it all?" I ask.

"I don't know. Too bad you don't have a fireplace."

We get out of the truck, leaving the headlights shining on the pile. The wood smells fresh and wet. Clair picks up a piece of the pine.

"It's going to have to dry for a while before I stack it in the shed."

Clair goes back to the truck and flips off the lights. The smell of wet pine seems to get stronger in the dark. My eyes adjust slowly. The quietness of the country folds in on me. The night sky is clear and crowded with stars, so many that they form murky patches; clouds of stars. The humidity, the dark, the quiet, the smell of the wood, and the stars—pinpoints of light reaching earth—are intoxicating.

Clair has lived out here for years, she's used to the country. It's such a contrast to my life in the city. I'm not sure I could live out here alone.

Clair is inside, she's switched on the back porch light. It illuminates the new white toilet she's going to install. The light also shines on a dead goose lying in the dirt, its long, elegant neck limp and twisted.

"Clair, you'd better come out here," I say, heading for the door rather than the goose. Clair comes to the door with her shotgun. She holds open the screen door with the toe of her boot. The shotgun rests casually at her side. It's not unusual for her to pick it up; there are plenty of stray dogs out here, the odd snake and potential prowlers. Clair's place is at the end of a road that cuts back and forth through the hills for miles. The last time she used the shotgun was the night we were followed home from the bar. We knew which of the drunken louts were behind us. Clair let them ride up close for most of the way, then, in the last set of turns, turns that Clair knows better than anyone, she took off, got inside, grabbed the shotgun, and blasted out one of their headlights as they turned into the driveway. They sat there for a couple of minutes, probably looking at the shotgun pointing at them from around the corner of the house. They ground the gears finding reverse, spat out a bunch of gravel, and whipped out of there. I was still in the passenger seat.

"What?" asks Clair and at the same time she sees the goose. The door at the back of the garage creaks open and slams closed. I start moving towards the house again, Clair is blocking my way.

"Who the fuck is out there?" she yells, practically in my ear. She shoves the shotgun at me, points to the toilet, and says: "Brace yourself. I'll turn on the lights in the yard."

I sit on the toilet, it tips over, I land in the dirt, falling

41

on the shotgun. I prop myself up on my elbows, stand the toilet up, flipping the lid down before sitting on it. Out from behind the garage, a man in gumboots and wet clothes staggers into the yard—a bottle of booze in one hand and a dead goose slung over his shoulder.

"Clair! There's a really drunk guy out here!"

I hear Clair calling the police.

"Tell him he'd better fuck off or you'll shoot him. I'm giving the police directions out here."

"Jesus Christ, Clair. I'm not going to shoot him. I'm not going to shoot anyone."

Clair drops the receiver on the kitchen counter. The screen door flies open and slaps against the side of the house.

"Fuck off! I've called the cops. If you don't want to get shot you'd better turn around and get the hell out of here," she yells.

Clair looks down at me. Legs spread, feet planted firmly, my back resting on the toilet tank. Clair lifts the shotgun barrel up. "You may as well point it at him and not the ground."

She goes back inside. The guy has stopped in the middle of the muddy yard. He sways, takes a gulp off the bottle, and flings down the goose with a thud.

"When I get a hold of you I'm going to fuck your brains out!" he yells before stumbling backwards and falling. He gets up mad and lurches towards me. I muster a faltering "Stop!" I have the shotgun on him, my finger on the trigger. "Clair, he's not stopping."

"Shoot. Take your time. Aim," she calls from inside, inside where it's cozy and familiar, where Clair and I sit and tell stories, where we laugh and drink beer, inside where I visit Clair, thinking about the contrast between the city and the quiet of the country, enjoying the dark and Clair's stories, inside where I admire Clair for her bravery and envy her independence.

He's lunging forward. The shotgun explodes and my arm smashes against the back of the toilet. He's in the mud. Clair is there saying over and over: "Fire another shot into the air." She grabs the shotgun from me and pulls the second trigger, blasting a shot over the garage. Clair reloads and sits on the steps. I start to get up and the toilet tips over again. The guy doesn't move.

"When the cops get here you're going to say you fired a warning shot and he didn't stop," she says. "He wouldn't stop."

I'm sitting in the dirt, my heart is pounding, I feel light-headed. Clair is calm. The shotgun is resting across her legs, she's rolling a cigarette. She strikes a match and a siren whines in the distance. A warning shot. The first shot. A warning shot.

The cell door closes behind me, it's a solid steel door, no bars. Both bunks are occupied, I sit on a mattress on the floor, leaning against the cool cement wall. I've been interviewed by the police, fingerprinted, photographed, and charged with manslaughter. I'm wearing baggy green pants and a pullover top that is too tight across my chest. The guard, a middle-aged woman with heavy eyeliner and antiquated blue eyeshadow, handed me a zip-lock bag of cornflakes and a tiny carton of milk—no spoon. I take a handful of the cornflakes and sip the milk. On the edge of the stainless steel sink there's a sandwich, one bite out of it. Bologna on white.

I slip out of my housecoat and pull off my leather aviator's hat as the room heats up. I wrench off my boots and set them on the table. I drag out the suitcase of shoe polish from under the bed. Hundreds of tins clatter. I've got polish in teal and peacock blue, jasmine and cranberry. I've researched all the companies around the world that make shoe polish and I have samples from most of them. I take out "moon grey" from Czechoslovakia and flip open the metal wing latch. It spreads easily over the curves of my boots, taking over the flamingo. I put them near the stove to dry and walk barefoot across the room, the dirt floor getting cooler as I move away from the heat.

There are paint chips embedded in the floor, all different colours. I tried to press in dried flowers too, but it seems like the accidental scattering, a by-product of some other activity, worked best. The flowers crumbled as I sank them. I wonder about things like that; accidental and overlooked beauty. There is a concern for walls that I find strange. They are supposed to be smooth, flat, and evenly coloured. I try to imagine the people who make walls, who fix walls. If the sea is the ultimate expression of darkness, then walls are the ultimate defiance of horizontal, inanimate life. Walls are ignored when they are flawless. It's usually only a damaged wall that attracts attention. They are metaphors, tactile boundaries. Their maintenance can be used like a textbook. A series of physical alterations of a wall is a formal repetition. History. History is one story, only one of the stories, the one that is closest to the desired surface. Walls should be clean, furniture should not mar them, putting nails into them must be carefully calculated.

I'm looking at something undiscovered, ignored, when I see the side of a building, the outline of a staircase where the paint and plaster have fallen away to expose a strange history.

It always seems to be the places that nobody controls or cares about where you find the best examples of hidden history. It's almost voyeuristic to look at something created by circumstance as having meaning or beauty. There is something intriguing about this phenomenon; it is impossible for me to knowingly create that state. If I have ever left something behind that was interpreted in this way I would not, by definition, be able to recognize it. If I value what I produce I've either lost or gained control. And so the spiral of darkness begins.

In the dark I feel my way down the stairs. I walk through the poplars and towards the heavier forest. It presses against me, as if someone is beside me. The branches creak in the wind. I try to stare at where they might be, but it's too dark. I'm trying to locate an object without light or sound. I lose my balance here. It's easier to see what is around me without looking directly at it. Looking straight ahead in the dark is confusing.

Walking back to the house I watch the tops of the trees out of the corner of my eye until the light behind the curtains is too distracting. The bathtub is glowing grey, it shifts and then reforms itself when I look away. In the dark the ground neither begins nor ends, it is not a solid thing.

The reiteration of simple stories is important. Stories about telephones and long nights of love are important. Stories about a man, a woman, and a car in Texas can be important. It doesn't matter what the storyteller meant to tell, in the end, it's what the listener understands. It is hard to be the teller of such stories; stories that are important beyond what was intended, beyond what the writer, the singer, the conveyor knew.

I used to be very careful about how I represented myself. I was responsible for everything I did and said. I learned that humour didn't translate well. No matter how clear I thought I was I noticed that I was still misunderstood. In fact, the clearer I was, the larger the degree of misinterpretation. I regained control by deciding that I could allow that to happen. Then I was in the same position. In control. In order to get beyond this I needed to explore the dark. I would like to work my way back from the darkness taking slow steps, breathing in everything I missed along the way.

I've been thinking about power. The dynamics of power and control, of a certain kind of blindness. Control is a convenience. Power doesn't disappear into anything, it can't hide, not easily. It's the worst when it isn't recognized, when it's put forth as part of the whole, accepted. It is a room in a house that has to be travelled through to get to the door. Some people languish there, in that room, developing an all-encompassing need to represent themselves with power. They are thinking about something else, but power propels them. Like the universe, it's impossible to think of the vastness of power. There are no systems to describe the dimensions of eternity, the distance to the end of time. It doesn't matter. Power has to be given the same absolute understanding and, simultaneously, the same disregard.

Perhaps control, the manifestation of power, is easier to grasp. Words are the tricks that force you to listen, they can force common thoughts to jump the voids to places where things can be rediscovered, or discovered for the first time. Words are a power vehicle for manipulation. Control. They are not innocent. Innocence is falling backwards off a bridge in a dream and waking up before you hit the water or the rocks. Innocence is a creation of power. It isn't real. It is the partner of power.

If you don't believe in yourself you will be faced with time. Waiting. To break the static patterns that wrap you in a binding hold you have to get used to a wavering of concentration; a relaxation in calculations. There is a theory attached to control, something like logic, a personal logic.

I am controlled by guilt. That's why I'm here, alone, trying not to wait. I've been the same person for as long as I can remember. I look at power and control because they alter me, as they alter everyone. I watch them, use them, and experiment with them. Mostly, I've been shaped by them. Power over me has created self-sustaining waves that travel through my life. Power re-creates itself in the people who have been subjected to it. The form it takes mirrors its original structure.

INVITATION MISTAKEN

My invitation to come over was explicit. When Ray arrives at the door he tries not to say much because he knows I'm trying to figure out how drunk he is. I know he's drunk when he says, "*I'm* not drunk. I'm *not* drunk. I'm not *drunk*," with hard inflections on each of the three words in the sequence. I let him in.

I walk across the room and his eyes follow me, watching the tops of my white stockings below a too short black velvet dress that moves nicely on my hips. I sit down and the dress pulls up even farther. I spread my legs slightly and he can't keep his eyes off my cunt. It's right there, for God's sake.

"I'm going to tease you, toy with you, just a bit. Tease, not torture," I say and he nods slowly, still staring at my cunt, grinning. This is a man who I take care not to hurt.

I'm touching my cunt and he gets down on his knees. I insist that he can only look. His tongue, a perfect pink bud, involuntarily pokes through his parted lips. I tell him, "No," but I let him lick my wet finger. He seems grateful. He says his mouth is clean but he could go brush his teeth. I tell him not to and he says it's the only way he knows how to clean his mouth. I say, "I don't care if your mouth is dirty."

He raises his eyes and finally meets mine. Reaching backwards to steady himself on his chair, he gets off his knees and sits down heavily. He feels around in his shirt pocket for cigarettes, lights one, and starts jamming it into the side of the ashtray before there's even an ash on it.

"OK," he says. "I understand. You've said no and I won't violate that."

He's drunk and probably can't get it up anyway. I feel uncomfortable; either over- or under-dressed. I inch up in my chair, closing my legs. He was invited to come and fuck me. Who could mistake me for no? There is beauty in not making it too easy for men to plant their heels on my chest and grind. I feel sorry for them, try to help them into my life, my mind, my cunt. I'm branded with pounds-per-square-inch tread-marks. At least a stiletto punctures and it's over. I'm pum-melled. I have a reputation for hurting men when all I do is love them and give them too much. I guess that's what hurts. Eventually I stop. I'm a practical person. I look good on a pedestal, I look good in comfortable underwear. Fuck the thong, I don't need something creeping around in my ass crack, I count on the world for that.

We've managed to feel rejected by each other. He admits he's probably too drunk and that he's not sure he has any condoms.

"Step into my sphere," said the lady to the guy.

"Don't send your sphinx my way . . . don't send your sphinx to town," he said.

It's a confusing thing when you believe in someone because you trust them. Fire comes with fire.

"Are we always drawing backwards?" said the lady to the mirror.

"Claudine, don't send your sphinx to town. You picked a fine line to wheel."

"It feels like 7 a.m."

"Then you've got another whole day," he said.

"No, you've got another whole day on that tiny little

stage you call your town. And don't worry, no one's following you around."

"Claudine, don't take your sphinx to town."

"Step into my sphere," said the lady to the guy.

He asks if he can come back tomorrow and he'll bring condoms with spermicide. I invite him for lunch and tell him regular condoms will be fine. He's insisting on spermicide. I'm trying to tell him that at this point in my cycle it's not necessary, but maybe later on it's a good idea. He keeps saying he wants to be responsible about this and I tell him, "I don't really want a bunch of chemical shit in my cunt every time I fuck, plus, I don't like the way it tastes."

This quiets him down and he goes out into the darkness. I hear branches snapping and his muttering as he tries to find the path.

The next day I am looking through clothes. I find a pink cotton dress with a rip at the neckline where the fabric has worn thin and come apart. I drape it across the bed. It doesn't suit me, it isn't my style. I unzip my jumpsuit and step out of it. I slide black stockings up my legs and get them into the little snaps, twisting awkwardly to do the ones in the back. I push my feet into black high heels and put on the dress which rips a bit more.

Half a bottle of champagne and his wine glass are on the table, I'm teetering around trying not to let my heels sink into the floor. Ray appears in the open doorway with a bunch of purple wisteria and weeping willow branches in one arm and another bottle of champagne cradled in the other. He laughs a little, probably because he's never seen me in a pink dress, but I catch the second when he notices what's beneath it. He turns his attention to wiping his feet on the mat before he steps inside. I try to take the champagne as he tries to hand me the flowers and we both laugh. He puts them on the table and hugs me. As he's hugging me he sees the two trout over my shoulder, one big, the other small.

"Nice looking fish."

I look back at the fish and say, "It's hard to catch two the same size. We'll have to do a little dividing up when they're cooked. Also on the menu is a dandelion salad and really tender little carrots."

"And plenty of champagne," he adds, filling my glass and then his own. We clink glasses and Ray sits down. He looks at me carefully, sets his drink on the table and says, "Come here."

I step towards him. He spreads his legs and pulls me between them slipping his hands up under my dress.

"Very nice," he says as his arms lift my dress up around my waist.

"I don't know if you're the type of man who likes to take a lady's stockings off or leave them on when you fuck her. I like it with them on," I say, smiling down at him.

"That'll be fine, just fine, but I don't know if you're the type of lady who likes to fuck before or after lunch," he says.

I laugh a little and start to pull away. He tightens his grip on me and, holding my dress up around my waist, he pushes me into the chair across from him, loosens the satin cord I'm using for a belt, and ties my hands behind me and then to the chair.

"I need something to tie your legs with."

"Right behind you."

He ties my ankles to the legs of the chair.

"It's too bad about the little rip in my dress, isn't it? I know it's just going to get torn more," I say, looking down.

In one motion he tears it to the hemline where he has to give it a solid yank before it comes apart completely. I push my cunt forward, up towards his mouth, spreading my legs farther. My heart is pounding, my breath trembling. He puts his mouth on my cunt, circling with his tongue, licking and poking. I push it at him and the ropes tighten.

"I want to suck your cock now."

He unties my ankles and helps me to my feet, my hands still secure behind me. He leans against the wall, I get down on my knees and pull at his zipper with my teeth. He pushes me off so he can get his cock out for me. I sit back on my heels, licking my lips. I put him in my mouth and rock back and forth, gliding it in and out, sucking it hard, circling the tip with my tongue. He can't take too much of this and he pulls my head back, holding my hair in his fists to keep me off his cock.

Ray tilts his head back against the wall. He's breathing hard. He doesn't want to give in too soon. He takes out a condom and slides it down his cock using both hands. I like to see a man with his hands on his cock. He leans down and slaps my ass. I fall sideways. He pulls me up and gets me onto the bed face down. He spanks me and I squirm, trying to roll over. I pull one leg up, almost getting onto my side. Ray takes this opportunity to shove his cock in. My wet cunt lets him in easily. My ass is stinging, my hair tangled across my face.

He stops fucking me, pulls out slowly, puts his cock near my face telling me to suck it. I open my mouth and he guides himself in.

"Stop sucking it."

I stop and he says, "Who told you to stop?"

I suck and stop in a confusion of commands until he

rolls me on my back and carefully brushes the strands of hair off my face. He gently works his cock into my cunt. He gets his fingers down and asks where it feels best to rub. He watches my face for answers, feels how my body moves in response. When I tense up to the point where I'm almost still, just on the edge of coming, he knows not to change anything he's doing. I don't have to direct him any further. My cunt clenches, throbbing on his cock. I moan, my head snaps back and he starts to push into me for himself as I'm coming hard. In his last deep thrust he groans and relaxes, draping himself over me. His hot breath fills my ear like the ocean roaring in a shell.

THOUSAND WATER RUNNING

I didn't come here to escape. I don't have any illusion about returning to something that never was. I don't wish I'd lived in any other time.

On the path to the beach I take a trail that goes off and uphill, eventually coming out on an open bluff above the sea. The grass has been flattened down by the wind. Near the edge of the cliff, angular black rocks form a ridge against the wind. I get down low against them and inspect the flecks of bluish-silver mica embedded in them. They shine even on the dullest days. The first place I saw the silver was on the rotting wooden sundial near the house. It had been carefully inlaid in an elaborate series of symbols. I'd tried to chip it off the rock in thin sheets. I wasn't particularly successful, but I managed to pick enough of it off to tap and rub into tiny triangles I'd etched into the thick green glass of the shed.

The sundial is a round of cedar mounted on a wooden stand. When I found it, it was almost totally covered in moss. I gave it a shove and the thing broke apart, exposing orange. I had to clear the moss off its surface to see what it was. The rudimentary designs were carved so carefully, filled with the mica. That's when I got the idea to try the same thing on the opaque glass. I was trying to get away from a devotion to intricacies, trying to get away from those kinds of thoughts—ornamentation, decoration—I wanted to forget those inclinations and live simply, but I was intrigued by the silver mica set into the cedar.

The name of the house is Thousand Water. I found it spray-painted on the cliff under vines. I call it Thousand Water Running. It's appropriate. I am looking at my bed, wondering about sleep and dreams. I sleep well at night, it's the time when my mind is most active. In the late afternoon I have long naps filled with the yes and no of guessing whether I'm awake or not. Those dreams are vivid and seem to be closely linked with my waking thoughts. Sometimes I solve problems in my dreams. People come and go with answers and suggestions. My dream at night is always the same, or at least, it feels the same. Every night.

When I lived in the city, traffic roared up on all sides. I lay in bed on a life raft in a terrible episode of survival, the survivor doomed to ride the waves without rescue. Ever-elastic vehicle, salted up, floating on my back, holding in salty tears, buoyant. Calm hostage begging: "When will my life begin?" I was weighed down, dragging an anchor of never-ending work, organizing a series of events that simulated life. I fell in stride with other people's lives, but I couldn't feel my own—built on deadlines, plane tickets, and reasons not to do anything new. I didn't want to be an eternal searcher. Where was my relief agent?

The dream I have every night is about last summer. It is one long segment; an accurate screening of my life from the day I left here to the day I returned. Like all histories it is selective, but I don't know what's been left out or what my mind has altered. It's a dream, not a memory, but having seen it unravel every night, I can't tell the difference. This is not what it's supposed to be.

I turn out the lamp and go into the extreme of darkness, always heaviest after bright light. When I lived in the city I stole light fixtures; small spotlights from unmonitored corners of nightclubs. I guess that's where it started, in nightclubs, where power is distributed in a pre-arranged contract. It wasn't a plan, it felt good. I had a collection of miniature tools, I figured out when I could do it, then I'd work away at it, throughout an evening, bit by bit, standing at the bar with a bulk of electrical components in my deep pockets. I thought about the filament, the cords, the thin glass of the bulb. At home I took them apart, bending metal with needle nose pliers, watching the fractures as they occurred.

I strike a match and light a candle, a candle that burns with a faulty glow. Soon it will sputter out altogether. This is the transition, a ritual of slowing down, frame by frame to stillness and sleep. I drape the blue wool housecoat over the curve of a chair and unzip my white jumpsuit. I hang it on the wall. The limp jumpsuit is only white where there isn't any paint, mud, or glue. The candle goes out. I sit down on the edge of the bed and pull off my boots. The sheets are cool against me as I slide between them. I hold my breath and think about the crackling of the last bits of wood in the stove. The heat propels the sound toward me. Let me tell you about last summer. Let me tell you about the trip to the source of the water and beyond.

AQUEDUCTS

I guess I'd thought I'd find a little stream or a spring. I climbed the cliff and pushed through the dense forest. I found a slippery green pipeline with a pile of bricks crumbling away at the opening. The opening was about five feet in diameter. I stepped inside and ran my hands over the bricks. The curves were as smooth as stainless steel. I felt my way along the inside of the pipe in total darkness. I heard water trickling under me. I wanted to stop and go back, but at the same time I felt compelled to go on. I turned towards the light and regained some strength. That was before I felt something more about the dark and its strength.

I picked up a small stone. I held it in my hands for a few minutes, thinking about fear. I rolled the stone between my palms and vested it with the power to keep me safe until I returned. I set it down and the current of water carried it, rattling, down to the opening of the pipe. Now I can hardly recall that fear.

The next section of pipe was down the other side of the mountain. It was too small for me to get into. I called down it and felt my voice shooting away from me into the distance. I'd expected an echo, but it was like calling out over the sea. I climbed back out of the pipe and followed it back up. I found marks etched into the brick, some kind of mathematical system. I found two more pipes running parallel to the first one, both snaked over with vines, both with the same markings where their diameters changed. The aqueducts ran across the valley and up the other side into the mist. I sat on my side of the valley watching the mist pull off the trees on the lower slope, but the hillside was never completely free of the dense fog. Far above the mountain the sky was clear blue. Where I sat the air was dry and scented with pine needles heating up. The valley below was defined in crisp light and shadow. I waited for the fog to clear off the slope so I could continue, but I became impatient and imagined I knew enough about what was under the mist. Twigs and needles snapped as I slid down towards the valley floor.

On the other side I made my way over mossy boulders and the murky pools of water trapped between them. I continued uphill and the mist blew around me, a surprisingly warm mist, almost steam. It was brighter than full sunshine. I crouched and rubbed my eyes. The mist was so dense that it obliterated everything. I felt around for footholds in the rocks and used roots to pull myself up onto a soft forest floor. I crawled along on hands and knees and felt warm water squeezing out of the moss under my weight. I came out of the mist and stood up beneath blue sky; steam rising and falling in waves at my knees. Five pipes, each one ten feet in diameter, ran straight up a cliff, a six-hundred-foot sheer drop. A waterfall streaked down the entire distance, disappearing in a haze of steam.

The strangest thing about this place was its desert climate. Even though it was saturated, the colours were warm orange, dry sepia. The cliff was sun-baked red.

I noticed the outline of steps cut out of the rock face leading to the darkness where the waterfall careened out of the side of the mountain. There appeared to be a cave up there, with a rainbow arching out of it. Attracted to the dark, I made my way to the base of the cliff and to the steps. A slack rope with a frayed end dangled through metal pins attached to the cliff face. A guide rope to the cave. Spray-painted in bright orange on the rock were the words: "Complexity Is The Ghost Of Understanding."

For the most part the steps were dry and cut for a leisurely ascent. My hands felt for the rope in the tricky spots and it was there.

ULTRA DROWNING

In the mental world of ancient systems, perception challenged belief. Doubt. The sender received the message to shift the claim stakes. Furthermore, the locks were changed at midnight. Standing in a lunar garden, palms flat, palms down, intuition tells me the concept of luck has just been dissolved. I hear the irons clanging from my last life, from the past. Forgery rings true. Fate floats on its back.

Contact me on mercury row, riding vapour pools. Fatality sounds more feminine than death. Address your revelations on the subject of death to the cluster of voices rising like a chant, "Ultra drowning."

The case before us involves the spiritualist's immortal body of tricks. In the evolution of the mystic, credibility is deceit.

"Ultra drowning."

The case before us involves the ultra drowning of the spiritualist's immortal body of tricks. The jury stands on a plate of glass above the prisoner's dock, looking down between their feet, past their flapping coat tails and blowing hems. Sound is piped in with a slight delay in transmission, the judge's lips move before the words are heard. Out of sync. The judge rarely raises his head.

I'm running with that conking-conk sound of water in my ears.

"Ultra drowning."

LOOKIE-LOO

I pin my eyes on my eyes in the mirror. I turn my head from side to side wondering what people really want to know about each other. He doesn't want to know how many men I've been with or hear about my fantasies. He knows what he likes. Black stockings. He has a thing about feet, not just my feet, but feet. I guess it's women's feet, but I don't know. It must be women's feet. I am a swarm of possibilities that make him feel either good or bad; that's all he needs to know. There's something I don't trust about the way he has sex. It's theatrical. A series of events occur in a familiar, publicly manufactured code. Passion is invoked by way of false memories, sex is an automatic formula. I turn into celluloid; simultaneously I edit and splice. It's not love that I don't feel, it's the loss of something that never was, something that may never be recovered.

If it's not an ocean, it's an island. Twisted in a dream, they feel like the same thing. I'm suspended by telephone lines. What am I looking at? Is it land or an oncoming wave? The guide boat capsized hours ago. My sea captain on shifty pins weathered a storm that didn't exist. Not so much steering as hanging on to a well-oiled wheel. I've been jolted to recalling a fear that aircraft can't and shouldn't solve. I've spent too long mending a rift that no one should know exists. A fear, buried in a half-dozen places. Shouldn't it be left for dead with these people who keep inquiring, politely, if they can re-invent themselves? The test control project thrived, the evidence

61

collected spawned a strain of concepts hitherto unknown or ignored and now the facts will survive.

Outside the circus tent, in a pen set up with flimsy sections of chain link fence, the elephant sways restlessly, back and forth, bending at the knees, ears twitching. The audience in the tent alternately gasps and claps as the trapeze artists go through their routine. The season is winding down. There are only a few more performances, only a few more times to pack up the tents, the scaffolding and the animal cages. The crew is tired, even the guys who hang around the elephant pen every night before the show are a little bored of it all now. Most of them have been following the circus for a month or more. These men have no interest in the show under the big top, they wait for Ray Lavender to come into the pen, secure the elephant with chains, and reach into its ass to pull out shit. No one wants to watch an elephant shit during the show.

Elephant Boy has more groupies than the ringmaster, more fans than the beautiful Russian twins who take turns putting their heads in the stinking mouth of the lion.

Ray phones to tell me that he can't stop making up haikus in his head. When I first told him about the haiku contest I asked if he'd write some with me. He said he didn't get it and couldn't do it. Now, it turns out, he can't stop. The contest deadline has come and gone, but I forgot to tell him. I forgot to tell him there should be a reference to a season within the haiku. He can't stop counting, he's using his shit-grabbing fingers to count the syllables in the elephant's ass.

Will you marry me?
There's comfort in knowing you
Will be going home

I called on my God
She is not answering me
What will I do now?

The sun is shining
I see your loving face
You're making me smile

My self-reference
Is boring the one I love
Now look she is gone

He was her lover
The stupidest man she knew
Sounded like music

The beauty of Claudine
Surpasses the rising sun
It makes my cock hard

I'm trying to hear
Your refusal to talk hurts
Give me a call soon

Claudine and Ray in bed
Playing with each other's heads
Loving love will flow

Ray says: "Steel toes and a mind of silk, that's me, alright."

I say: "Well I'm one of those weird ones who prefers to think while I talk. I had a line, I had a line that I forgot. That can happen when I think and talk at the same time."

"Oh well, equal time for irreverence. Hey, what's the best thing a human can do for mankind?" he asks. "Show them love?"

"There are a lot of different solutions to the general demise. Be loved," I say.

"So, are you a witch?" Ray asks.

"No, I just got behind in my work. The blocks are always up and you'll never know what you're being tossed," I answer.

"I don't know, I always get cautious around women wearing Satan rings."

"Never mind! He's a cute little guy. How tall did you think Satan was?"

"Don't heel me just to break me. I'll leave me for you. Some people want to see God, some people have to be God. I am, too!"

"At least I know you're listening," I say, taking a gulp of beer.

"Hey, where's my beer? Mona Lisa, Mata Hari, Yoko Ono, Emma Peel, Angel Avocado, no sleep dreams. Hey, there's the 8:57 gun. Are there Messiahs waiting in the wings married to their hair? Look, I'm walking on the beach on Mars, I'm a farm boy used to hanging off the bumper of a truck. Give me a break!"

Ray and I are on the bed. He is lying on his back, I'm sitting next to him showing my camera. I haven't had it out of the drawer for a few years. It broke in New Zealand. I was told at a camera shop that it wouldn't be worth fixing. There are two things I never try to fix myself—watches and cameras. And anything to do with computers, of course, because I have learned, patiently, to hate them.

The camera is a small, expensive, 35 MM Rollei. It moves easily in my hands. Holding it, explaining the elementary functions to Ray, brings back memories. Ray bought a camera from a guy who sells stuff from unclaimed storage lockers. A Nikon for forty-five dollars. But it's an automatic Nikon. It's ugly, like most cars on the road, it's indistinguishable from other dumpy, rounded off, and ugly cameras. The elegance of older cameras has been sacrificed to make them super user-friendly.

Ray wants to take pictures of me. Posed, "Smile, say cheese!" pictures. It's very sweet, but I'm impatient. He has bought the wrong speed of film, he's got me with the late afternoon sun over my shoulder, and I'm thinking too much about something I'd rather not be. When it's dark he brings the camera out again and sets the flash. It goes off randomly, accidentally snapping a picture of the canopy of catalpa flowers above us, which might actually be a pretty good shot. He winds the thing, pins me in the viewfinder and it flashes before he touches anything. He figures it's something to do with the mode button. Mode. Every oversimplified piece of once easy to fix machinery seems to have a mode button on it. The answering machine—the one I have to listen to to find out some crucial detail from all my messages from the last week—has a mode button. The fax machine that cuts off the answering machine in the middle of a message has a mode button on it. The microwave must have one too, but I've never gone near one to find out. So, it's the mode button on the Nikon.

I'm struggling to explain the Rollei in sequence. "It's

65

more labour intensive, or rather, thought intensive, than a full size 35MM. Because it's compact you don't look through the lens to focus. The lens, when not in use, fits inside the body of the camera. Push the release button and it pulls out with a beautiful rushing sound of metal on metal. The considerations are then examined. Because you look through a viewfinder rather than a lens you have to calculate distance, speed, and aperture. Then you look at the ring around the lens to see your depth of field related to your aperture setting. At a distance of twenty feet with an aperture setting of eight, everything will be in focus from ten feet to infinity if your light meter is lined up right. I usually do that with the shutter speed. Unless I've got a moving subject, then I work on the speed first."

"Do you have the book that goes with it?" Ray asks.

"Yes. Why?"

"So I can figure out how to use it and take some pictures of you with it."

It probably only seemed like a long time before I said, "I'm not lending it to you."

But within that time I thought about doing the research before I bought it. Trying out other cameras, talking to photographers, listening to my mom say that she didn't think the man I eventually married had much talent—now, almost twenty years later, he's still a full-time photographer at the city's largest daily paper. I thought about sacrificing the ability to see through the lens to frame my subject: to visually focus. I could see a black-and-white face moving in and out of focus ever so slightly. I found the point where the eyes, or maybe just one eye, twinkled back. I remember going to Granville Street to take carefully planned shots of fruit and flowers outside markets. I can see myself, strangely enough, from the other side of the street, a young woman with long hair falling over her face, looking down at the camera in her hands, figuring out how to get what she wanted. I still run across the contact sheet from that black and white roll and I feel the self-consciousness of really wanting to succeed. Shadows languish across voluptuous melons, every pore of their water-colour paper skin in focus. A silently questioning tiger lily peers into the camera, gazing astutely from a swirling blurry mass of petals, stamens, and stems. Once I've said it—"I'm not lending it to you"—it doesn't feel right. I add to it, backtracking, "It's kind of complicated."

I can practically taste the disappointment spilling over rolls of machine prints picked up from London Drugs on lunch breaks. The questions, "What happened here? Why did it do this? How come? . . ."

I would like to not think about the answers.

"It's a complicated camera. You don't just point it and shoot. You have to want to learn to take photographs."

"What's the matter with pointing and shooting? What's the matter with an automatic camera? Why not just capture the moment? Isn't that better for most people?"

I believe Ray has picked up on my preference for a single lens reflex 35MM camera that doesn't have "mode" stamped on it.

"Well, it's like any art form, it takes work and it seems to me people are getting farther away from understanding what they're using. Now that self-serve gas stations are everywhere people don't check their oil or tire pressure as often, if at all. The garage guy used to do it so now it just doesn't get done."

"Lots of people don't have cars," says Ray.

"Most people around here have access to cars, it's just the people you know who don't have cars. Should everyone who picks up a guitar be regarded as good a player as you when you play it all day? What's the matter with working at something? Or should we all forget it and watch TV or sit in front of a computer on the internet, instead of actually interacting with another actual human being?"

"I don't even know why we're talking about this."

It makes me sad to think of the desk drawers in "most people's" homes, overflowing with photo envelopes that encourage them to buy more film. Happy snapshots of little girls in floppy hats, all windswept and tanned at the beach. I mean it. It makes me sad to think of the photos in albums with cellophane over them that eventually get too crispy to hold the pictures in place. The pages turn and the photos slide across. The rings of the binder don't allow the cardboard pages to turn easily. These albums have "My Photos" embossed in gold on their plastic covers, the same kind of stuffed plastic that some people prefer for their toilet seats, which, by the way, also makes me sad. If that's the extent of luxury one demands, then I am truly far away. If I rented an apartment with a padded, pillowy toilet seat, I would unscrew it and prop it up against the garbage cans for some lucky soul to claim as treasure. I don't replace my toilet seats with oak, I just accept the standard issue plastic seat and dream more elaborate dreams.

I know I'm the one who's out of sync. I learn about "most people" because they're everywhere, I'm just not one of them, but sometimes I wish I was (or is it were?). I'm forever on the outside. I only hear about the neighbours dropping by with bottles of homemade wine to sit on the back porch admiring the ingenuity of building a trellis for the zucchini as well as the grapes and, "Ya, it worked out good. The slugs don't get 'em so bad."

I come from a place where the air practically has to be par-boiled before you can be bothered breathing it. Mostly I feel like I'm on the other end of a phone line from where "most people" microwave new-improved-pop-tarts and the automatic drip coffee starts with the alarm clock. I can feel every inch of that plain white string stretched tight between two tin cans. On the other end I can hear the dog's too-long nails scraping slowly across the kitchen linoleum, the kind that's rolled down in a sheet and trimmed with a knife under the counters before the stove and fridge are moved back in place. In the background I can hear a simple comment designed to be universally inoffensive.

"She's a hot one today."

"Yup, sure is."

Back in time, back to the country, back to a place I'll never get to. I'm an onlooker, a lookie-loo, a voyeur with what's-his-name's story of the eye cruising around too close, too close.

I have a plastic groom from a wedding cake propped up against the window, hands clasped, I suppose, to cover his erection. His hair is brown and pressed tight against his plastic head à la Ken awaiting his Barbie's hand, elbow, shoulder, down her back to her thigh. From outside I see the groom has a handmade, thrift store price tag: twenty-five cents.

Dear Ray,

 I'm at a motel, by the pool, near the highway, in the sun, just outside Houston. I can see you doing all sorts of things. The packet of sugar rips open and the tomato glistens as the grains liquefy. I can see you getting the coffee ready—me sitting in my chair. Sometimes, being on the road, it seems like the struggle to find my toothbrush never ends. Time is an awkward reminder that there's plenty of waiting around, but never the kind of time I need to relax in myself or have anything in a familiar system or formula to accomplish very much.

 Playing was fun last night—I got some good guitar sounds, but it was a weird scene; depressing, but we got through the set. I'm letting the watery shapes that tremble across the pool relax me as I think about your philosophies. I feel like I examine life too closely, with too much concern for what is simply average and normal. I lose the thread of my own set of philosophies because I try to ignore them, believing I'm leaving myself open to letting more in, but that then turns into what I am: some weird observer who cannot escape subjectivity. I am a conduit for understanding basic human nature, but I am a poor chronicler of it on my own. Chronicler. Is that a word? Somehow that reminds me of a conversation I had in Germany with Bubu. "What is the difference between 'corner' and 'corner'?" he asked over and over, until I finally realized he was saying "corner" and "coroner." Dave had a conversation with Dirk about "character." Dirk was trying to understand what a "corrector" was within a person. He also thought that in a U.S. court there is a person called a "prosticutor!"

 No one can escape subjectivity. I wonder why I even care about what people think; not so much in relation to me, but just to know what they think about, to understand. Texas might not be the worst place to lose faith in people, but then what shall I do? People here don't seem to question too much—there is "is" and there isn't a place for me except outside "is." There are too many people trying to be the next weird thing. That is almost as tedious as trying to be the next big thing. I'm OK—I'm just struggling with being a voyeur on a voyage, observing while I'm being observed. There is almost no calm place to think on tour. I hope this sounds like me in your heart. I'm just trying to be the usual me.

     Claudine

FILM SHOOT

Three buses pass me, all full, but I don't mind. It gives me more time to talk to Ray. He's waiting with me, smoking nervously. I'm on my way to a film shoot. I've only told Ray a little bit about the part I'll be playing. It's a small part, but he heard enough details for him to ask me not to do it.

A bus pulls in. I kiss Ray on the cheek, touch his arm lightly, and climb on. When I get to the address—an industrial park outside town—I pull open the mirrored door and sit down in reception with five young men reading magazines. A call comes through the intercom:

"Send them through please, Nadine."

Nadine wheels herself back from her desk, stands up and opens the door to the set. One corner of the room is a beautiful bedroom suite—like something off *The Price Is Right*. The bed is huge. It's covered in quilted white satin. The furniture is dark and sensuous. Around the foot of the bed there are 35MM cameras on tripods, lights, and reflector umbrellas. The director starts telling the men where to stand and Nadine leads me off to wardrobe and make-up. The wardrobe girl has a huge blonde afro and long fake eyelashes. She's wearing thigh high black boots, leather shorts, and a frilly lace shirt. She asks me to undress. I was told to wear loose clothing so there wouldn't be any elastic marks. I pull off my t-shirt and sweatpants. I'm naked. She asks me my shoe size. I give her my clothes when she puts out her hand for them. She puts them on hangers. I don't think I've ever hung up a t-shirt and sweatpants. She starts flipping through a rack of lingerie asking me if I have a preference for lace, leather, or latex. Almost everything is black. She hands me a latex garter belt and a heavily constructed, very low-cut bra. I wriggle into the garter belt while she looks for stockings. I start to put the bra on and she turns to help me.

"The director likes a lot of playing around with tits," she says. "He'll probably tell you to take this off. He'll be happiest when you're on your knees, shoving your tits at the camera. Pull and twist your nipples, act like it's really driving you wild to play with your tits." She laughs a little bit. "I know it's ridiculous."

I look in the mirror.

"Here, put your leg out and I'll roll these stockings on and you'll be ready for make-up."

I put on pointy-toed high heels and follow her out into a well-lit, triple-mirrored make-up booth.

"Take a look at some of these girls and see what kind of a look you want."

I flip through some porn magazines and decide to go for big red pouty lips, heavy black eye-liner, easy on the blush. I ask her to tease my hair up and out all over.

"Since I'm here I may as well play the whole thing out."

She laughs and sweeps heavy foundation over my face. I follow her instructions to look up, close my eyes, open my mouth, press and rub my lips together. She back-combs my hair so hard that my head snaps around with every stroke. The results are dramatic—I don't feel like me anymore. I've been transformed into one of the girls in the magazines that lie folded open and dog-eared amongst the clutter of make-up tubes and brushes.

"Let me do your nails real quick and then I'll go tell them you're ready."

She's fast. The only thing to slow her down is the cigarette ash that drops onto the just-finished nails of one hand.

"Shit. Give me your hand."

She wipes the affected nails with polish remover, stubs out her cigarette, and re-applies the polish. I sit with my hands resting on the arms of the swivel chair, turning my head from side to side, practicing the looks I'd tried in the mirror at home. Head back, neck muscles relaxed, eyes slightly closed, mouth slack and open as if to say, "What the fuck are you doing to me? I've never felt anything so good in my entire life!"

I blow on my nails and develop the attitude that I conjure alone or with my more adventurous, not so easily threatened lovers. Some men seem to find the over-the-top sexuality that they jack off to with pornography a bit much in person. They don't know quite what to do with an aggressively submissive woman.

The intercom buzzes near me and a male voice says, "Nice work, Claudine. We're ready for you on the next set."

I push away a box of tissues and find the speaker. I notice that one of the mirrored panels has a different density to it. A one-way mirror. I begin to wonder how much control I have over this situation. This must be an addition to the script. I slide off the chair. The latex garter belt squeaks against the plastic seat. I look at my ass in the mirror. There are red marks from sitting. I start to rub them and remember the camera behind the mirror. I feel myself becoming the character I'm playing.

The light on the bedroom suite is warm pink, the film cameras are invisible behind a border of darkness. Male voices are whispering, laughing softly, trying to create enthusiasm. I take the glass of champagne off the nightstand and sit down on the edge of the bed.

"That's right, Claudine, have a few sips and relax. You look beautiful and I want you to show the camera that you know you're beautiful. I know you've never posed before, but you're going to do just fine. We're here to make it easier for you. When you're ready we'll start off with some simple shots 'til you get feeling comfortable."

I'm not sipping, I'm gulping, refilling my glass awkwardly, wishing that they'd given me a bigger one. I shiver involuntarily and try to start playing out private moments of extreme lust. I lie on the bed and watch someone who looks like me in the mirror on the ceiling. I squirm on the cool satin, transfixed, my movements in sync with the image in the mirror. I'm all tits and hair and red lips and clit bound up in stockings and black rubber. My eyes have adjusted to the darkness and I can see the film crew behind the guys with the 35MM cameras. I put two fingers between my legs and then into my mouth.

"Let's get a shot of you on your knees facing the camera," the guy playing the director of the shoot says. "Take off your bra and rub your tits."

I pull myself to the end of the bed, unsnap my bra, and hold onto the tall bedpost with both hands above my head. The flashes and clicks of the cameras are co-ordinated with my movements. I rub my clit on the bedpost and watch myself in the mirrored wall.

"That's great, Claudine. Now look back at the camera and pull on your tits. Give me that hot look I saw earlier."

One of the guys standing around is rubbing his cock in

his tight jeans. I part my lips and moan, rubbing my breasts, squeezing my nipples.

"Fuck. Fuck. Fuck," I say over and over, each time I let the word take a complete exhalation of its own. The guy standing by the reflector umbrella has taken his cock out of his jeans. His belt buckle dangles heavily on his thigh. He starts to move towards the bed saying, "Fuck, she's wet. Get her hands tied behind her back."

Another guy, taking his shirt off, moves toward the bed. They put me on my side facing the camera and tie my wrists. They roll me onto my back. One guy straddles my face and puts his cock in my mouth while the other one fingers me. I can hear my wet cunt, juicy on his pumping fingers. I moan, my mouth full of cock.

The film camera is down close to the bed on a crane. A guy wearing headphones holds a boom mic over the bed. The actor with the 35MM camera is on the other side of the bed firing off shots, close-ups of the cock going in and out of my mouth, close-ups of fingers going in and out of my cunt.

"OK—I want some fucking now. Take turns, keep one hand on your cock when you're not fucking. OK—Claudine, where's that 'fuck-me-hard' look? Come on—you're loving it! Open your mouth, put your head back. That's it!"

The film being made is about the filming of a woman who arrives to do a photo shoot for a magazine spread and the crew just can't resist her. I'd read the script five times before taking the part. I'd liked the way the film revealed something cold and calculated about pornography. The film exposed the woman as an actor, an accomplice rather than a victim. The woman knows all along that there is no photo shoot, but rather a film about a photo shoot and the actress—me—knows that it is a film about the filming of a photo shoot.

"Claudine, look at the camera, sweetheart. Good! OK—I want her face down, ass in the air, keep her hands tied behind her for a finish-up fuck. Take turns."

My face sinks down into the white satin. One of them, I can't see which one, tries to put his cock in my ass every time it's his turn, but he's too big. They each come with pounding thrusts, holding me by my hips, my ass shaking with the pumping.

GIVE ME A HUG

Ray is standing in the kitchen, naked, leaning on the counter.

"Give me a hug," he says.

"No, you're all sweaty. I hope you don't mind taking a nice bath with a woman floating around in it with you."

"No, I don't mind at all," he says.

I reach over and hold his cock, weighing it, squeezing a little.

"Look, it's so small and shrivelled!" I say, smiling. He knows I like it that he can be so compact in contrast to the size of his erection.

"Oh thanks," he says in mock irritation. "I love hearing how small my cock is."

I look at his eyes. He looks worried. "Anything wrong?" I ask.

"Well, yes."

"What?"

"Star phoned the house today. She's coming to town tomorrow and she's staying at my place. My uncle said she could. She got some kind of cheap ticket from a friend."

"Great. So just like that she's coming out and staying with you."

Star and Ray lived together for ten years until she ran off to Ottawa. Ray went after her, but she never came back. Most of Ray's songs are about her. He sings them every day. He waited seven years for her to come back to him. His songs say there is no other, he'll wait forever, he was Adam, she was Eve. It's hard to go to his shows. He plays in strange restaurants where most of the tables stay empty all night. I sit dutifully, drinking beer and listening to him, but before he gets too far into his set he's lamenting Star, how he wishes she'd stayed, how he misses her every day, he'll be here waiting for her for as long as it takes her to return or at least give him a call. That's when I start to feel self-conscious and I look out the window. Sometimes Ray's friends look over at me, thinking they're love songs about me. I shake my head. My friends look at me wondering how I feel about these endless songs for Star. So she'll be here tomorrow.

"Did you want to use the phone? It's about 8:30 in Ottawa," I say, trying to be calm, trying to accept this. His face brightens and he moves towards the phone to tell Star he'll be waiting for her, or that she's welcome to stay as long as she likes, or what?

"Would you mind putting your pants on to call her? I don't really appreciate you calling her up with no clothes on," I say, wondering if I'm being silly, wondering where I fit into this, wondering why Ray doesn't ask how I feel about it, wondering why it's OK with him to have her stay at his house for a week, wondering why she's coming out, what she wants. Ray is in a hurry to call, to tell her yes, it's OK.

I walk outside, sit on a stool, and tap my foot slowly in a puddle, watching the ring of water move away to the edges.

"She's not coming after all," Ray says, stepping outside. "She can't use the ticket and she might have to move."

At least now I know that without warning, without any time to get used to it, Star can phone, arrange to stay at Ray's, and be out here the next day, and everything will be fine. Even after seven years it was a big deal for him to tell her that he had fallen in love with me. She'd said, "You can't have!"

Ray and I get into the bath. She's not coming. I try to relax, drink my beer, and shut up. I can't.

"Why is it OK for her to arrive on a moment's notice and stay at your house?" He dismisses my emotions and I resort to my usual technique of setting up an analogy.

"I don't think anyone would be very comfortable with this."

It seems like he can't understand my emotions and he has to find ways to say what I am feeling is wrong. I'm not mad, I'm hurt. I don't want to say I'm hurt by this, I don't say that. I don't want to say I'm afraid, I'm scared, I feel threatened, that this makes me feel insecure. I say, "I think this is inappropriate. You still love her, your songs are about her—about you and her being together. She can just drop into your life and that's supposed to be OK with me? I'll never be as good as Star. I'll never be as beautiful, as young, and you'll never love me as much as you loved her."

I feel betrayed, worthless, unimportant. All Ray can do is challenge me. "You got a fax saying you could tour in Australia and you're talking about going down there," he says.

"What does that have to do with anything? That's my job and by the way I invited you. I'm trying to get your CD put out, I'm trying to set up a tour for you. What does that have to do with this? Don't even bother! And, by the way, if she does come out, I'm not sitting around some crappy restaurant with her while you're singing a bunch of songs about how much you love her and want her back! I'm sure she'll be there lapping it up. In fact you can just go off and be with her if she shows up, she'll be staying at your house so you don't need to be hanging around here. I'm sure I don't even need to encourage you. I've never fought for a man and I'm not starting now. You've never told me anything about her other than she was a waitress in a restaurant where showing off her tits was part of the job. You explained that she left you totally out of the blue—which says to me that you weren't noticing much of anything. Other than that, I don't know anything about her."

"Why would I tell you anything about her?" he says. "You don't want to know her, you don't want to meet her." I can tell how protective he is of her. She needs him, she knows he'll always be there for her, he needs to be there for her.

I get bent into being someone's woman to find out he's someone else's man. Dedicated forever. Ray gets dressed for work, to sing his Star songs, and I just don't feel like going to listen. I lie in bed for hours, adrift, alone, lonely, blaming myself for imagining that I ever thought I was someone special, but at the same time feeling more and more like me.

He comes over late. We were going to go to a party, but I don't feel like it. I don't have anything to say. I'm not interested in making everything fine and alright and good again.

He seems a little grumpy that I'm not going on about it. It's late and he's not saying anything. Eventually I ask if he's just going to sit there saying nothing.

"I'm waiting for you to say what you're thinking," he says.

I don't have anything to say except, "What are you thinking?"

"Don't you think it's possible to love someone and then love someone else?"

"What do you mean? That you love two people at the same time?"

81

"No," he says. "You just don't like it that I ever loved Star."

"That's nothing I've said and it's not true. You're just trying to start this thing up again. And I don't like being told I've said something that I haven't."

Eventually, after he's tried to make feeling lousy my fault, he says he loves me and not to worry.

THE BLACK WEDGE

In the mid-eighties Mecca Normal released its first LP on our newly formed record label, Smarten Up! After that we flew to Montréal to hook up with another voice and guitar duo, Rhythm Activism, who were also dealing with social concerns from an anti-authoritarian perspective. While the four of us stood around in the basement of the CBC building, waiting to do a live, Canada-wide radio interview, we listened to the broadcast in progress, which featured England's Red Wedge. Formed in the late eighties to support the Labour Party, the Red Wedge presented political ideas within a musical context, a showcase of musicians encouraging people to vote Labour. That night, the Black Wedge came into existence, to encourage people to reclaim their voices, to speak out against oppression rather than rely on electoral politics as a means to solve problems.

We phoned Vancouver and a bus was secured for a west coast tour. The tour lineup included Mecca Normal, Rhythm Activism, Ken Lester (D.O.A. manager, activist, poet), Dave Pritchett (longshoreman and poet), and Bryan James (a self-described "jingle man"). Gary Taylor, our driver, wrote and read his first poem on the tour.

Leaving Vancouver after a sold-out show, we headed south, playing nightclubs, an anarchist bookstore, an art gallery, a soup kitchen, a record store, universities, and as many radio stations as possible along the way. Our preliminary promotional work paid off and articles appeared in many publications, including mainstream newspapers.

The show, divided into five segments, dealt with a variety of issues. Mecca Normal performed "Strong White Male," "Smile Baby" and "Women Were King"—all of which deal with sexism and male oppression. We also performed "Are You Hungry Joe?"—a dialogue between Joe, a guy in a Toronto food bank lineup, and the guy that stood between him and a bag of groceries. Rhythm Activism also addressed poverty in "The Rats." Bryan James' songs were about pornography and the lure of the TV screen. Dave Pritchett's poems were mainly about disenfranchised citizens and lost love. Ken Lester's poems were in the Beat tradition.

Between songs and poems we all talked about what we were trying to do with the Black Wedge. Sometimes it sounded dogmatic and rhetorical, other nights it was spontaneous and charming. In Olympia, Rhythm Activism's Norman Nawrocki called for a raid of the Safeway next door—it didn't quite happen, but there was enthusiasm for the plan.

We are driving to Zurich through the green hills of Bavaria. We have to go through Austria to get to Switzerland. I did not get enough sleep. I was at the disco until late. I am in the back of the car feeling sick. We cross the border, I start to feel better. This is the beginning of the tour. Dirk is in charge. I am nervous, I'm not used to following someone else's idea of organizing a tour. Dirk is driving fast, pulling right up behind cars and then darting out to pass. He says he used to be a race car driver. I relax.

It is dark when we get into Zurich. Along one street

there are hundreds of people buying heroin and shooting up. We are zeroing in on the club, weaving through narrow streets. The place turns out to be a squat. It looks like a movie set. Weird construction, barricades, wild paint, and sculpture make up the front of it. We walk into a courtyard and are taken towards a hole in the ground that leads down a rickety ramp into the cellar. There is a bunch of machinery with pipes and gauges all over the place. We feel around in the half-light, dragging our equipment with us. The stage is floppy, like cardboard. We bounce on it to see where it's strongest. The Swiss technical guys watch this bouncing carefully. Before we can do a sound check they have to re-wire the amps to make them compatible with their power supply. I decide not to wear a dress and start to wonder about the rest of our tour.

The squat has been around for over a year. They try to keep the drug scene out. We are taken on a tour of their concert hall, a disco, a café, a bar, a used clothing store, and various living spaces. The empty building next door has been taken over recently. Fences and barricades are being put up quickly because they're expecting a battle with the police over the new squat.

Munich is grey. Everything looks fine at the club. We walk around the corner to a Bulgarian restaurant. Dinner is definitely the highlight of the evening.

When we return to the club for sound check I start to get the feeling that there is a problem. The PA has only one channel and there are no monitors. This is a big club and we are the only band going on. The PA guy is trying to rebuild a three-prong microphone jack by twisting wires together, his hands are shaking, he is making excuses. He sticks the jack into the one channel board and gets a loud drone. We still have hours to go so I tell him to get a better set-up. He returns with another board and we do a quick sound check before we start. I find out later that the sound was not coming out of the main speakers. The only audible vocals came through the monitor facing me.

While we're playing I'm noticing a certain amount of disinterest, but that gradually changes. We're about five songs into the set, both playing guitar wildly, when the PA guy comes up on stage and says we can only do one more song because the manager hates us. I announce this to the crowd and go into the next song. As we're finishing, the disco booth operator puts on a record. I am definitely not done. Neither is Dave, he has just pulled his amp to the front of the stage, turning it up loud. The microphone stand goes flying off the stage, someone picks it up and puts it back for me. I yell, "Fuck the management!" into the mic. The disco music goes off and we continue for another song. The PA guy skulks back on stage to relay the message that we won't get paid unless we stop now. I tell the audience that gas is expensive and we are finished. They seem to be on our side. I push through the crowd towards the door. The place is packed. I introduce myself to Frank, the manager, and tell him he's an asshole. This conversation goes on for a few minutes. I make my point and he wants me out of there. Dirk appears and goes into the office to get the money. We are told to leave the club immediately. There is a lot of confusion at this point, getting the equipment off stage and through the crowd to the sidewalk. We pack everything into two cars and go in search of a bar.

Sitting at a smoky table, drinking beer, not under-standing a single word of German, I feel very alienated; really lousy. I find out that the disco booth guy had pushed Bubu when he'd gone up to tell him to turn the record off. Also, the manager said we drank too much of his beer.

I go with Rainer and Bubu back to Kaufbeuren. The tape deck doesn't work so they are singing songs along the way. I am curled up in the front seat, sleeping on and off. I wake up when we pull into a barnyard filled with people. Bubu slowly weaves between them, gravel crunching beneath the tires. People bend to look in at us. It is raining. We park and go into the huge barn. We buy fake American dollars and get in the lineup to buy two-dollar beers. Rainer buys a little cardboard boat of potato noodles which he ends up wearing on his head. The sound system is huge.

There is a smoke and light show to go along with the Abba songs.

I look for a place to lie down.

JEAN: So how did you get started doing this, Calvin?

CALVIN: I'm trying to do this in a creative way. It might be easier to use processes that other people have established, but I guess I am resistant to stepping into any process until I've proven to myself that it is the right process. In a way I'm always re-inventing the wheel because I'm rejecting the industry standard, or at least I'm not adopting it immediately.

JEAN: When you're interested in a band is it the idea of working with somebody who has a similar method or vision and not necessarily a particular sound?

CALVIN: Right. For instance: Mecca Normal. The first time I saw them was on the Black Wedge tour where they got together with their friends and said, "Hey, this is important, let's do it." It wasn't as if they were saying, "How can we sell this new album?" It was a tour of people and half of them weren't even bands. It was incredible.

As a group, the Black Wedge was grappling daily with the same concepts that, nightly, we pontificated about from the stage. In San Francisco, Bryan and I published a small newsletter called *Bus Tokens*. We distributed it that evening at the show—to which only a handful of people came. I was the only woman on the tour and Bryan is black; the rest of our tour mates were white males. In a somewhat frustrated tone *Bus Tokens* railed against authoritarian sexist attitudes on the bus. As a group, we presented a show to inspire people, to introduce the possibility of creating poetry that was aggressively useful and music that was stripped down to the powerful basics of guitar and voice, but as the tour evolved and we became more frayed, and I became more aware that we had created a microcosm of what we were expressing opposition to. I think people who address social concerns are expected to be beyond reproach. With the Black Wedge tours and subsequent politically-based endeavours, it became clear that there was no purity in this type of work. There was no path laid out in front of us, mistakes were made, experience altered our approach. Once you start a project you forget about the beginning, you're too busy dealing with the stream of problems and opportunities that follow. I wish more people would find a way to begin.

Tonight it's a youth centre. A guy named Scarlet O'Hara is putting on the show. We find the place despite the kooky squiggles we got for a map. There are some really young looking guys on stage tuning up really loudly. The PA has to be kept low for two reasons, it feeds back if it's loud and the shows at the centre are driving the neighbours crazy.

While the opening band is doing their sound check I manage to lock myself in the bathroom. The door is steel, the handle is loose, the window has been boarded up. I look in the mirror, my face is white, my hands are shaking, I am dizzy. I kick the door and finally the music stops. I yell for help and someone comes to the door. I ask him to get my friend Dirk, and he goes off calling, "Dirt!"

When I get out I am ready for a beer, but Dave says they don't have beer at youth centres. I walk out to a dark street and look up and down for a store or a bar. I don't see anything that looks open. Back inside, Dave is opening a beer for me. Yes, they do have beer at the youth centres.

During the show there is a lot of drunken pushing and yelling. When we finish a woman who has been huddled on the edge of the stage rocking back and forth yells, "Come here, baby!" at me and I head for the opposite side of the room. The first person who approaches me is very enthusiastic about telling me how much he didn't like us.

The crowd staggers away, stealing some of our beer, and we are left with Scarlet, the guy who doesn't like us, and a guy in his fifties who says we are all going to his Portuguese restaurant for salad. Gee, I could really use a salad right about now.

The restaurant is dark. The owner unlocks it, turns a couple of lights on, and disappears to make salad. Meanwhile Scarlet is talking about having us play in Portugal. Two shows a day on the beach for the summer: $10,000.

We are told that the guy who doesn't like us will be

taking us to his place to sleep. I do not like this guy. I don't like it that he's at the restaurant let alone that I am going to his place to sleep. When we get there he becomes very animated towards his dog, his cat, and his bird. The bird bites my finger and he warns me, "Be cautious, it's a woman."

He takes the dog for a walk and we use the opportunity to phone Scarlet and tell him we are coming to stay at his house. It is the middle of the night and we can hear the guy walking back up the street with the dog; he is whistling, chirping, and barking.

Almost ten years later Rhythm Activism's Norman Nawrocki says, "I used to be a journalist, but I made the switch to electrified alternative journalism" with his band—"a rebel news orchestra." Along with Sylvain Côté on guitar, Nawrocki has reported on poverty, housing, racism, the union-busting policies of Coors, violence against women, and the Zapatistas of Mexico—devoting an entire CD to this subject.

In a recent battle over tuition hikes, Montréal students contacted Rhythm Activism to help counter unjustified anti-student propaganda.

"Friday we wrote 'Fight The Hike,' Saturday we recorded it, by Monday it was blasting out of speakers on the picket lines at four universities with students singing along from photocopied lyric sheets."

In 1990, during the seventy-eight day stand-off between armed Mohawks and federal troops near Montréal, Rhythm Activism released their *Oka* cassette in support of the natives. "The Mohawks played the tape on speakers directed at a few thousand troops," says Nawrocki. "College radio right across Canada played it. It inspired people to join in and, in some cases, to set up support groups for the Mohawks."

Rhythm Activism has a reputation with the media for responding to news events with biting commentary. "During the Gulf War," says Nawrocki, "CBC International phoned to see if we had released anything about the situation. We released the *War Is The Health Of The State* cassette within the week."

CALVIN: It's hard for things to change if people aren't going to exchange ideas, if they're only going to say, "If you disagree with me then you're the enemy." One thing that's really useful when discussing issues, especially issues of repression, is to see all the different points of view and try to understand why someone would look at something as repressive while someone else doesn't. Not to say that one person is right or wrong, but to understand why that can exist.

JEAN: To want purity out of every situation is an antiquated idea. It is totally language-based—having everything succinctly packaged, allowing no ambiguity to leak in at all—I don't think there is a reality where that exists.

CALVIN: Extreme points of view are also very useful because so many people are trying to avoid conflict. The great thing about rock 'n' roll is that because it is a three-minute song you can get one idea across. That's important. Artistically it seems like so few people are doing anything interesting, taking risks, changing or adding anything. I see a lot of changes in your music. I see you adding things and subtracting things one at a time, slowly over a period of time, and it's really interesting. Whatever you're doing at any one time is fantastic. It works as a whole, it's complete, it's not like a work in progress. That's exciting and it's exciting to meet other people who are doing things like that, but a lot of times those people aren't well understood by the people who are just consumers of media, consumers of music. They're just like, "Oh, entertain me." It's kind of sad when people who are doing something that is different get to the point when their different thing becomes the accepted thing.

In 1987 the Black Wedge got on the same old school bus and drove from Vancouver to Winnipeg. On the bill again were Rhythm Activism, Bryan James and Mecca Normal, along with Mourning Sickness, who were "committed to destroying all forms of patriarchal power," and Peter Plate—"an agent of the spoken word" who had seen our San Francisco shows the year before and decided to join us. Responding to an ad in *Open Road*, an anarchist news journal, Nelly Bolt took on the driving. She also set up a literature table while Mecca Normal's David Lester put up a display of political posters at every show. Booklets containing a selection of everyone's work and a compilation tape had been sent out to secure shows. One promoter in Edmonton cancelled our show after hearing Peter Plate's piece "San Bernadino"—in which someone jerks off on a church door handle Saturday night so his dried seed will touch the priest's hand Sunday morning.

On a ferry trip across a lake in the interior of British Columbia, Peter Plate climbed onto the roof of the bus to deliver a poem without warning. The other passengers tried to pretend this wasn't happening; people in cars rolled up their windows. After Peter was done, most of us got up there and yelled out poetry to our captive audience. I think it was Nelly Bolt's first public performance!

In Toronto, Prudence Clearwater was attacked by a man on the street. On stage that night she was so strong doing her rant against street harassment. "Listen to me, little man!" she howled down at the audience. It felt like our introspective world of touring had been interrupted by reality.

One of the last times I saw Prudence she was climbing out of the overhead baggage rack on a Greyhound after an overnight trip.

In '88 Peter Plate and Mecca Normal went to England to perform on the cabaret circuit. We were sandwiched between highland dancers, comedians, and skits. Peter was dynamic, all his pieces were done from memory. Mecca Normal has always wanted to be either a contrast to a larger, more traditional rock forum or, as part of the Black Wedge, an element within a similarly motivated group. In England the other acts were entertainment—something we've never wanted to be!

After the tour ended I stayed in the north of England doing some readings and running a women's writing workshop which was set up for me by Keith Jafrate, a poet, a sax player, and an employee of the local council. He was running writing workshops at all different levels involving poets and people interested in improving their writing skills. Keith gave me a lot of opportunities to stay in England and work on my writing. In '89 Keith joined the Black Wedge tour in North America. He teamed up with Rachel Melas on bass and we were joined again by Peter Plate. We toured the west coast and the northeast before the thing exploded for financial and personal reasons. That was the last tour that I know of called the Black Wedge. The name is, and always has been, for other people to use to present anti-authoritarian ideas. It is meant to be an arena for people who might not otherwise be known well enough to bring out an audience. It was never meant to be a closed group that was only active for a short time.

Bicycles are moving throughout the city, at the end of a journey they are left for the next person to use.

Prior to the Black Wedge, Mecca Normal had not toured at all. That first tour was amazing; we met poets, community activists, anarchists, feminists, people at radio stations, independent record label people, fanzine writers, and bands. At that time we had no idea what was out there. It wasn't nearly as connected up as it is now. It was incredible to drive into a community on the bus and see what was going on, and at the same time, represent ourselves. After the group tours—five Black Wedge tours—Mecca Normal became more insulated, preferring to tour by ourselves and play on regular rock bills as a contrast to the four guys on stage syndrome.

JEAN: Do you think longevity becomes a political thing? You're continuing on with K, we're continuing on with Mecca Normal. Is it a political point to put other parts of your life aside and relegate yourself to a lifestyle that doesn't have much to do with glamorous financial success?
CALVIN: The way I look at it, there are two parts to your question. Is rock 'n' roll just a youth thing that you should stop doing at some nebulous point? The other part of the question is—what is the motivation of an artist who looks at a life's

work rather than an arty period in their life? I don't really look at art or music as something that should be ghettoized to a certain age group. That's something that we've always emphasized since we started. We want to have all-ages shows, shows that are not restricted in any way. That includes old as well as young.

Have I ever told you the story of the bird that wouldn't fly? He asked time and time and time again. He kissed her hand. He asked if he could touch her. Time and time and time again. He's guessing now. You wouldn't believe it—the story of the bird that wouldn't fly. He kissed her hand. He's guessing now.

If the Black Wedge shows themselves were not consistently well attended, we did get air time and press—not only at college stations and in leftist publications. We did interviews on national radio (Canada's CBC and England's BBC). Regional glossy magazines published photos and mainstream papers ran features. We felt that pushing our anarchist ideas into mainstream culture was important and we succeeded. The headlines read: "The anarchist Black Wedge spreads the word." "Anarchist poetry to the fore in war against social injustice." "Paint it black!" "Black Wedge strives for the subconscious." "Feminist aggro in the Black Wedge." "Wedgies are back!"

GHOST, GUEST, HOST

The altitude, in combination with exertion, was making me dizzy. I held onto the rope at all times now. I began to think strangely. I kept hearing someone asking for my knife and I kept saying that I was using it, couldn't he see that? I had the sudden realization that I knew where blue and orange came from and what they are used for. It was like discovering the information needed to solve a great secret. I laughed out loud, fell away from the cliff, and dangled on the rope until I swung back in and regained my footing. Even that seemed funny. I laughed again, but now with tears in my eyes. I climbed on all fours and watched a spectrum of colour fragments blur around me. I was almost at the level where the waterfall confused the entrance to the cave. Wind-blown splashes in front of me turned the soft steps bright orange where the drops hit. Hot salty water splashed on my face. The last section was a ramp under the waterfall. Overwhelming vertigo forced me to lie flat. I pressed the side of my face against the ramp and tried to make my whole body contact the solid rock. I felt like I was floating up, defying gravity. The trigger, the words on the wall, "complexity is the ghost of under-standing," the idea that I was trying to piece together a history on a preordained journey without a time frame confused me. I couldn't stop thinking about the word "ghost"—a subject in time, what's left after life, something not entirely accepted, maintaining a fragmented personality, drier and less whole-some than when it occupied its original life. Ghost, guest, host.

A transmutable embodiment of nothing. I twisted my head around and pressed the other side of my face against the rock. My eyes were clenched. On a cliff edge, in the heat, in a strange confusion, I wanted to understand; I wanted the history of darkness. Invoking accidental double negatives, I was still fighting perception in favour of belief, but I could sense an opening for perfect calm and renewal of strength and courage moving towards me, waiting for me to make the choice; how would I proceed? Next I was struck by an overwhelming sense of certainty. I had believed the world to be one way and now that view had been altered, not eradicated, but added to so convincingly that everything was thrown into question and I trusted this perception immediately. I wasn't looking for a reason not to.

I crawled in half-vertigo, semi-paralyzed, towards what I could see and smell and almost taste. The darkness behind the waterfall. The surface was slick and I went in with a final force, a reserve, through a sheet of light multiplied in a split-second regeneration of conductors. An explosion of light, then dark. I lay on my back, panting and wet.

Propping myself up, resting on my elbows, I looked into the light. The waterfall was motionless, but roaring, freeze-framed like an ocean crashing in wave-lengths on the shore from thirty thousand feet up. The cavern behind me roared an echo of extraordinary power. Cold air pushed down from a shaft above me, forcing the steam to separate and roll back into itself.

Standing up, I felt grit on my hands. Holding them to the light I saw they were covered in broken sea shells. Chips of mussel, flaked oily mother of pearl, barnacle edges, the scalloped ridges of clam shell and tiny cross-sections of moon shell spiral.

I'd followed the pipeline to vertigo and now I was in a steaming cavern beneath a rope ladder.

I stepped onto it and waited until I stopped swaying. The climb was awkward, I bumped against the walls as I worked my way up. I felt a blast of cold, wrapped my fingers over the edge, got a solid grip, threw my leg up, and hoisted myself onto hard packed snow. I stood up and slithered around on my smooth-soled boots.

I wasn't sure what I was looking at, the only things moving were the swans and the smoke. The swans were up out of the water, picking at their feathers. The parts of the water that weren't frozen were glacial green. Thick paste. Still. The snow was strewn with ash blown from hissing geysers of smoke and flame. It seemed random, widespread. Some places were untouched, then fifty feet away there was another fire. The snow looked like it was burning. No one was there, but I wasn't the first to arrive. At the time I couldn't really have said for sure, but now, in my mind's eye, I can see black footprints tracking through. The swans were cordoned off on ice.

RUSS MEYER, MONTANA

G iving up my apartment seemed brave and somehow glamorous even though it was because I couldn't pay the rent. I drove my '72 Impala to Seattle to hang out with a friend. I arrived at CB's, let myself in, ate her roommate's dried cherries, and rolled the district's name, Queen Anne, around over and over again as I walked through their spacious apartment thinking, I could live here, I could live here.

CB got home from work with a stack of videos. Russ Meyer, horror films, biker chicks from hell shot from ground level slamming the kick-start thing, leaving a cameraman in a cloud of dust. I hated them all.

"Let's drive to Montana," I said.

"Should we? Shit, I should get Bob's gun off him," she said, wringing her hands.

"You can't wear that. Or anything like it," I said, looking at her pink angora sweater and black leather miniskirt. I grabbed the remote and muted a vampire.

"We'll need egg salad sandwiches and the Christmas angel to keep us safe," she said.

I rolled my eyes and went out to the car for the map. Montana looked farther than it sounded like it should be. I checked the tire pressure. CB checked the fridge. At our first gas stop out of Seattle, CB bought tiny frosted doughnuts and set the box on the dash under the Christmas angel swinging from the rear view mirror. I shook my head disdainfully at the doughnuts, but fifteen miles later popped one and then another in my mouth. CB twisted and rolled around laughing.

"Wicked girl," she crooned.

We spent the first night in a campsite. CB wanted to pull over and sleep at the side of the road, but I wouldn't. She slept in the backseat, I slept outside and woke up at dawn with a thin layer of ice on my sleeping-bag. Swans clattered across a small lake, breaking the ice in front of them; the least graceful swans I'd ever seen.

I started a fire and made a little wooden tripod for my espresso pot to sit on. While I was brushing my teeth, waiting for the bubbling to begin, I heard a thud and sizzling behind me. The tripod had caught fire and dumped the coffee. Time to wake CB up. She embarked from her veritable suite, refreshed, asking about coffee. CB has porcelain skin, short dark hair, and the ability to look ready for anything wearing no other make-up than a streak of bright red lipstick. The black leather motorcycle jacket and tight black jeans didn't hurt, either. The only article that seemed out of place was the pair of horn-rimmed glasses without the lenses. They only got us into trouble once. We'd stopped for sandwiches, more egg salad sandwiches, at a bar. Some biker guy started asking CB where her motorcycle was. I was on the stool next to her, listening to her nervous story about being Isabel, visiting from Paris. The Hell's Angels guy leaned closer, noticing that her glasses were fake, and I think he began to feel he was being toyed with by these city girls. French, no less.

THE PUBLIC KNIFE

I could make out half-sunk pylons; braided wire sizzled and sparked around them. Grey paint peeled off the pylons where the flames hadn't touched. A single geyser of water jetted fifteen feet up like an uncapped oil well, blowing apart in the wind. Cold air sank around my feet, swirling in an icy mist. I followed the footprints. They led to a low, crudely cut archway in the glaciated cliff. Steps descended around a gradual curve. The walls of the passageway were ribbed, serrated. I ran my fingernail into a surface not much harder than wet clay. The steps turned into a carefully hewn cobblestone path. I was in a narrow canyon, just wider than the span of my arms. Angular, stunted pines clung to the rock walls, ivy tendrils reached down from the forest above. Warm air funnelled towards me, disrupting my sense of climate, season, and geography. Then, ahead of me, in the middle of the path, I saw something so familiar it made the hair on my arms stand up: a sundial, elegantly curving up from its obelisk foundation to its open whale's eye surface. It was in perfect condition, larger than the one I'd found and broken; it almost blocked the path. The cobblestones were cut neatly around its base. I put my hands on the surface and felt the inlaid shell fragments—purple mussel, oyster pearl, ridged clam—and the same silver that I'd found on the bluff. But it wasn't a sundial. The designs were elaborate and asymmetrical. A code. A story. A history depicted. It was a marker of some sort; a tribute, a warning. Its marks weren't meant to monitor time.

Cedar bows, scratching against me, were pushed back by a gust of wind, revealing a trail leading off the path. I walked along it into a poplar grove, blue sky above the swaying branches. I found about twenty more markers in the tall grass. The patterns and designs on them were all different, but they shared common themes. Along with the arabesques and scrolls there were horns and tongues, scales and wings, waves and clouds. The wood was deep red-gold, oiled to a dull shine. I stood still among these entities, histories, reminders of characters and accomplishments. They seemed to be the diagrams of lives. I was mesmerized until it struck me—these were the things that I had willfully destroyed.

I stumbled back to the main path and kept walking. I came to a wooden table with a spigot in the rock wall. A small sign over the bloodstained table read, "Whoever uses the public knife will let the others know if the knife has just been sharpened." A leather sheath was nailed to the sign. I took out a crooked blade and ran its dull edge across the ridges of my thumbprint. A stainless steel bucket was beneath a hole in the cutting surface. Crows circled above me and then, one by one, they came and landed on pine branches that bounced with their weight. They regained their balance and started to gargle and bray, stretching their bodies out like the prows of elaborate ships. Blue-black feathers loosened and re-tightened, eyes darting everywhere except directly at me.

BOB DYLAN AND CARUSO
AT THE LAKE

My mother is old enough to be my grandmother. My grandmother was old enough to be my great grandmother. She was Victorian. She died the summer I was two, the day I fell off the horse on the island. A horse, not a pony. No one seems to remember who put me up on a horse. My grandmother taught singing in New York City at the turn of the century. Horse-drawn carriages, long, mud-speckled dresses. I have a cotton petticoat of hers that I unfold every now and then. She sang in prisons to entertain the men. She saw Caruso sing in New York. Caruso is in the dictionary, on the same page as Casanova. Bob Dylan said, "I'm as good a singer as Caruso."

Her name was Anna. She married John, who let her go off to New York to sing.

My mother's brother, Uncle Vaughn, was a tough cookie, an authority on everything. He shaved with a straight razor sharpened on a leather strap, and he drove with both feet—one on the gas, the other on the brake. He was a pediatrician and could be expected to arrive at our house with advice and medicine.

Once, Uncle Vaughn decided to give my brother a lesson in toughness. He held him by the arms and dangled him over the cascading water of the Cleveland Dam. I ran like hell.

My mother speaks of her childhood with images from her mind's eye. From her attic room she could see the coal man, the ice man, the vegetable man arrive at the gate in the back lane. During the Great Depression men would come to the door and her father would invite them in for dinner. When my mother brought my father home for dinner for the first time, soon after they met, my grandfather accidently called him by the dog's name: "Please pass the butter, Pondo."

My mother was a star athlete, my uncle an academic star. While he was at university he built a chemistry lab in the basement of their house. I have the case he made for his microscope. I keep love letters and dishes of rings and necklaces in it. It is an amber wood box with an iron handle. It locks with a fancy little key. At one time in my life I wanted to live out of this box. I wanted everything I needed to fit in it.

My parents weren't young when they met. They were introduced to each other at a party thrown by someone named Fortune. My father was an artist and that was OK with my mother even if he was from the wrong side of town. He grew up above a drugstore. When my mother was a young woman she worked at a library downtown. My father used to go to that library to look at all the art books; he had no idea that you could borrow them and take them home. Worlds apart, those two.

Every summer my mother's family took the train up to D'Arcy at the south end of Anderson Lake. They stayed in a cabin on the far side of the lake, rode with the Indians, hiked in the mountains, canoed on the lake. They smiled in black-and-white photos; smiled self-consciously in awkwardly rolled-up trousers or half-wet bathing suits, shielding their eyes from the sun, heads tilted at angles.

One summer evening, at dusk, when it's difficult to see, a plane came down low over the lake and got caught up in the dizzying sheen. The plane plunged into the lake. My mother, a very young girl at that time, was playing with her dog on the beach. Her brother ran out of the cabin, dragged the canoe down to the lake, and hopped in. The dog followed him; my mother followed the dog. There was no time to get them back on the shore. My uncle paddled furiously out to the half-submerged plane. The cockpit was underwater and inside, trapped in suspension, were a bride and groom. Tuxedo tails and white satin floated around them. A wedge of cheese and an empty bottle of champagne bobbed against the inside of the plane. The pilot had managed to get himself out and he stood on the side of the plane yelling at my uncle to get the little girl out of there.

Uncle Vaughn lived back east, in Montréal. His wife, my aunt, was a non-practicing dermatologist. She had never practiced. It seemed one thing for a woman to actually get through medical school in the forties, but quite another for a married woman to work, especially when her husband was a doctor. I only met her a few times. Once, just before we got in the car to go to Cleveland Dam, I came running home from school to see them. It was very exciting! My aunt and uncle coming from Montréal for a visit! She stared at my feet and noted quite coolly, "I see we're both wearing Hush Puppies."

That was instead of "hello" and a hug.

She was a woman with a family. This was a formal family with property, some kind of mass burial plot in the right cemetery and a name, a way of doing things that was beyond reproach. She came from a family with money.

When they visited there was always talk of the lake, their lake back east. Up to the lake, the house at the lake, trying to get away to the lake. My brother loved this shit. The money, the class, this "up to the lake" business made him giddy. I could never visualize the place. I didn't like lakes much anyway. Still water stagnating. No tides retreating to leave rock pools of starfish, anemones, and barnacles. I was oblivious to the status and unable to conjure a cottage, a cabin, a hut, or a house by the almost motionless lake's edge.

This past summer Uncle Vaughn died up at the lake. He had gone out for his daily swim and died. When my mother called to tell me the news she seemed unclear about whether he'd died in the lake, on the way up to the house or inside. As the days went by she talked about their childhood at Anderson Lake. She still didn't know if her brother had drowned, had a heart attack or a stroke. She set the scene in her mind's eye for all the possibilities. Dredging the lake for the body, pulling it up over the side of a boat. Or seeing him clutching his bare chest as he fell to his knees on his way up to the house. Maybe he'd had a shower, towelled off, dressed, and sat down for breakfast. She probably had breakfast visualized, too. Face first into a plate of scrambled eggs.

"Mom, why don't you call out there and find out what happened?"

"I don't want to bother them, I'm sure they're upset."

"Of course they're going to be upset, but he was your brother, you should find out how he died. You're going to have nightmares about it."

"The family will be arriving and I don't want to upset anyone."

"Do you want me to call?" I asked. "I don't mind upsetting the family."

She called and found out that they'd gotten him into an ambulance but they'd been unable to revive him. It looked like his heart. Uncle Vaughn was in his eighties after all. Family, friends, and people who lived around the lake were going to meet in Notre-Dame-de-la-Merci, the closest town, for a small service to mark his passing. Some of the people from around the lake might not have known Vaughn personally, but they'd probably heard of him. People like that know who their neighbours are, especially when their neighbours are a couple of doctors.

It turned out Uncle Vaughn had slowed down in the preceding few years. He'd still made his rounds at ths hospital for sick kids, but he'd been spending more and more time up at the lake.

I didn't know whether to visualize evergreens or deciduous trees. There were crows in my head, and the motel where my mother and I would have stayed looked like the amber wood microscope box with black rectangles painted on it for windows. It was just far enough away from the house that we wouldn't have upset the family.

OYSTERS

Further down the path, now sand and crushed oyster shell, I could feel the sea. It was starting to get dark, the sun setting ahead of me, beyond a seagrass ridge. The path sliced through smooth hills and opened into a courtyard of creamy sandstone cliffs into which windows, doors, rooms, balconies, and staircases had been carved. Tiny yellow lights flickered irregularly, strung zig-zag above the courtyard. It seemed like they could go out at any moment. The windows and doorways were totally black. The sea's echo was a constant roar. I walked towards the sound although I couldn't tell, in this confusion of walls and rooms, where the exit was. I turned a corner and stepped onto a weathered boardwalk and the echo changed to the distinct sound of waves crashing, one after another. I walked on in the half-light. A woman carrying two wicker baskets was coming towards me. She was slightly off balance, as she got closer I could hear her laboured breathing, almost in time with the waves.

"I like your hat," she said, practically panting as she tried to get past me.

I pressed myself against the handrail to give her more room, but she plowed into me with one of the large baskets.

"Can I help you with that?" I asked.

She paused and leaned against the rail opposite me.

"Thank you."

I took one basket and she took my arm as she stepped down onto the shell path. Under the yellow light I could see her face more clearly. She had high cheekbones and the skin across her temples seemed translucent, blue veins were like rivers there. Her pale orange hair bunched up on her shoulders.

"I'm fine from here," she said, taking the basket from me. The cloth covering it pulled away and I saw it was filled with oysters in the shell. We were standing at the entrance to a narrow alley, at the end of it there was a torch in a sandstone gargoyle's mouth. She looked down the alley, paused, and asked, "Actually, would you help me inside with these? I'm more tired than I thought."

I took the basket and she motioned for me to go ahead of her. I walked towards the sputtering gargoyle and came out into a tiny courtyard. Wisteria tumbled down from the balcony above. A fountain in the form of a fish with wings was dribbling from the only gaping mouth in the courtyard. The water had made a slimy stain down its elegant belly. Lily pads were awkwardly propped up in the shallow pool, half out of the water. She led the way to the door and said, "Wait here while I find some candles. Put that down, it might take a while."

She put her basket down and somewhere in the back of the house I heard a crash and then a small light came on. She appeared in the doorway with a lantern.

"Come in, come in. And bring those baskets."

I picked up the baskets, went inside, and waited while, one by one, the corners of the room were illuminated.

"I'm sorry about the mess. Here, let me clear a space for you to put those down."

Every surface was cluttered with chipped, mismatched plates, cups, and saucers. Oyster shells towered in the corner, their opalescent surfaces undulating in the unsteady lantern

Kircher's view of a cavern being supplied with sea-water.

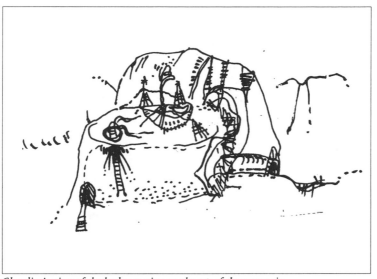

Claudine's view of the hydro station on the top of the mountain.

light. She shifted an entire section of dishes with her forearm, only stopping when plates started falling off the other end of the table.

"With the electricity off and that generator sputtering along as if it'll give out any minute, I'm trying to get as many oysters canned as possible. The boat doesn't come for another three . . ."

Her voice trailed off. She straightened up, raised the lantern to illuminate my face, and asked, "How did you get here?"

I squinted and turned away from the light.

"I came over the mountain."

NOTES

Missing information, ideas to develop, connections that need to be made:

Link the concept of a journey, a physical journey, with the journey to resolving conflict. The dilemma of the book is turning into the writing of the book.

More description of the power station, the characters, the shed filled with letters. More examples of letters written by the people who have visited the settlement and subsequently written letters to the ghosts or spirits after they've returned to their regular lives.

More background information on the theory of hydrology throughout history. Include description of water forced through subterranean channels "created by God in his divine wisdom—just like the veins and arteries in the body of man." Caverns in mountains are supplied with sea-water and in some cases the water is heated by underground fires, distilling it, getting rid of the salt. It appears on the surface in the form of springs and rivers. Include Kirchner's view (from the 1600s?) and the sketch from the top of the mountain. Insert information about how electricity was created at the settlement.

Re-write the sex scene on the film set. Convince the reader that the woman is not a victim, but a willing participant, that her fantasy is shaped by prevalent male fantasy and pornography to an indeterminable degree.

Power. Electricity was created at the bottom of a ten-foot dam on the creek. Evaporated milk cans had been cut in half to form cups, then attached to a large wheel. The water travelled through long tubes of wood. Many strong jets of water hit the cups and the wheel turned. It was attached to a pulley and belt which was attached to a generator. This created enough power to run a refrigeration system and lights.

Sound and light are linear systems in the physical world. Their electrical counterparts—the light bulb and the tube that produces sound through speakers—are also linear. A tube amp utilizes direct current. It takes alternating current and turns it into a one-way current—direct current. As AC flows back and forth through the filament (cathode) to the second element, the plate (anode), it produces DC current. AC is converted to DC. The third element is the grid—a coil of wire that allows electrons to pass through it. It is placed between the cathode's positive voltage and the plate's more positive voltage, right in the path of the current. The voltage on the grid is the bias voltage, less positive than the cathode. The more positive the grid, the easier it is for electrons (current) to pass through to the more positively-charged plate. If too many electrons hit the plate in an amplifier tube the plate glows and burns out; the grid has to be able to regulate the flow of electrons. The light bulb's flow of current allows the filament to burn and create light.*

Linearity seemed inescapable, its presence seemed to come on stronger than ever when I tried to defy it, to sneak around it. It made its case more convincing, another link along the way was established and solidified. The linearity of logic seemed to be irresistibly simple, even if the parts that lead to the whole conclusion didn't add up; it was a satisfying journey. Calling something logical weighed heavy on the side of infallibility. Logical: correctly reasoned, but not necessarily correct or true.

* Note: Paraphrased/taken from Geoff Farina in *Tape Op* (www.teleport.com/~fboa)

RIOT GRRRL

During the media frenzy that surrounded the women in rock thing I made myself available to journalists as a continuation of a policy I already employed. In 1993—a Riot Grrrl year—I did about sixty interviews. I had done the same number five years earlier and the subject had been the same: women in rock. In 1988 a Montréal paper quoted me: "My concerns involve the battle between men and women in our society. There are very few women in music and even fewer who sing about sexism."

In '93 journalists wanted to know why they were denied access to the individuals involved in Riot Grrrl, but they didn't like the answer. For the number of times I was asked this question the answer almost never appeared in print. Evelyn McDonnell's *Billboard* article was an exception. I was quoted: "The media are playing a significant role in misrepresenting these bands, or these women, or the concept. I could sing about anything at this point and people would say—that's Jean Smith the feminist singing about some further tragedy in her feminist existence."

Medieval man tucks the gun, tucks the gun of a calibre I'm not familiar with—I've never heard of a .33 automatic weapon—tucks the gun into the waistband of his tights and pulls his tunic down to stroll the room. If you know, if you know what a gun can do for you, then you know that the knee can produce a reaction in a jerk who won't shut up. Press the gun, press the gun on his knee, and talk to him. Talk to him. When the candle flares in a draftless room I can only assume it's the gasoline on your breath. Sammy, Dean, and Brian all became addicted to the farm gas barrels, the fumes. Medieval man knows that when the bricks end in a tourist town, you're on the outs, and the pace just picked down.

Inspiration stole my livelihood away, so I had to lie and say I'd never be the same. There was a time when I could not stick paste to paper and then I realized that was never the point. All about the same thing, it's all about the same thing.

If, and I do mean if, I say, "There's a sway to the way the wind blew today and all the cue cards were put down," if I say, "I saw a sparrow," and I may have seen a swallow and I'd only seen a swallow, it doesn't mean I'm wrong, it means I'm trying to be profound.

In '92 I was contacted by a producer of the Jane Whitney show—tabloid TV out of Boston. I was invited to participate on their "Women In Rock" program. I was assured that it was to be an unedited forum—a calculated reaction to Riot Grrrl concerns about media manipulation. Within the week I was flown to Boston from the west coast, put up in a four-star hotel, limo-ed to the set, and coached by producers to interrupt other guests. They'd tried to plan a little surprise for us feminist types by including an "MTV Girl"—a regular in videos that require tall skinny blondes rather then ugly musicians. She revealed her presence at the hotel, phoning me to explain that she herself was a feminist of sorts and planning to put out an album, "Like an Andrew Dice Clay thing, but for girls." She more or less asked not to be ripped apart. Personally, I had no interest in talking about her or her activities and I certainly wasn't going to stage the cat-fight the producers were after. By the end of the show she'd managed to embarrass herself (all by herself) with her endless self-promotion.

The show had been steered, in advance, towards the topic of profanity in rock. Studio audience member Tim Alborn of Harriet Records (and a history professor at Harvard) told me later that the audience had been jacked up on doughnuts and warned that us girls ran foul at the mouth perpetually and that we didn't shave our legs! That seemed to raise the level of animosity in the audience before we even got a chance to open our dirty little mouths. We were, in a Kafkaesque way, on trial. During the blank spots where commercials would be inserted, our make-up was smeared around while the producers swarmed around, encouraging us to reveal our personal victimization. I disregarded the direction of the show and talked about the absence of an adequate medical system, homelessness, the virtually unchallenged maintenance of an electoral system that doesn't offer choices, the increasing gap between rich and poor and the absurdity of a nation that fiercely defends its constitutional right to freedom of speech, but covers its ears and squawks when it hears words it doesn't like—not even ideas, just words! Most of this was cut from the broadcast of their "unedited forum." Now it's impossible for me to watch TV talk shows without sensing the behind-the-scenes shenanigans.

An interesting part of the relationship between the Riot Grrrls and the media was the more the Grrrls said they wouldn't talk, the more attention they got. The energy and potential surrounding the inception of Riot Grrrl—the movement—was replaced by an identifiable group of insiders with an agenda: refrain from talking to the media. The point when leaders become visible and members start responding to what's expected of them is usually the point when a good idea can start to look like an elitist organization.

"It was so long ago," says Bratmobile's drummer Molly Neuman of her experience with Riot Grrrl and the media. "When Bratmobile was playing, everyone was so skeptical and antagonistic about the media, but I liked it because it somehow legitimized the work I was doing. Now that I'm older and publicity (at Lookout Records) is my job, any and all press seems to at least serve some purpose. Also, now it seems like there is so much competition for attention and it is harder to get press when you're not a cultural phenomenon."

December (summer) '93
Dunedin, New Zealand

Dirk,

Well it is now December—December 1—so it must be time to write to you. I've been here two weeks now. I'm waiting for summer, but it is grey and windy. I was met at the airport by my new boss who happened to be coming in at the same time on another flight. I was a little too tired to meet the boss after flying for about twenty hours. Nothing is really that different here, mostly it's just kind of frustrating to do anything and of course I want to do everything and the wind is blowing the wrong way for that. It seems like no plan lasts longer than an hour and I'm not so deep in a million collision courses a day. Today, after I'd just gotten used to this old typewriter (fixed, dusted, new ribbon), the boss buys a new electronic one and suddenly I'm not such a good secretary (drinking beer and complaining), on a collision course with technology, and I remember why I walk alone and this city is not my home and I'm not alone in not my home.

Next day

I'm trying to remember how I thought this would all be here. My first job is to figure out what in hell is my job. On my second day here I was sent out to buy envelopes and my head just about exploded. Dirk, I'm not a very good envelope buyer! I can book tours, make records, write books, but I did not come to NZ to buy envelopes. Yesterday, after failing at everything, I went to play loud guitar. I tried to turn on a lamp and the light bulb sailed out. This was not the switch for light, but it must be the one when you need a light bulb on the other side of the room.

The first week here BB was downstairs recording and he kept coming in here to use the toilet. One night we had the door locked and we were in bed and there was knocking on the door—at first a little knock, then a lot of knocking, and then he kicked the door in, smashing the lock! He has quite an important bladder, I suppose.

I had a dream last night—huge human chess pieces were walking all over, up and down the stairs, no chessboard anywhere. I was on a bus going around and around the city. A guy with a big rubbery face was laughing at me and I pulled his hat down over his face. I had a tiny little dog for a friend, but the dog kept getting smaller and smaller until he fit in my purse. Then I closed it.

Jean

December '93
Dunedin, New Zealand

Dear Dave,

Things are not as I have let them appear to be. Do you ever wonder where the me who tells all the stories went? Well, I assure you, there are plenty of unsent letters around here. I still think you should come down and we should still do the tour, but I'd better fill you in on what's really going on here. More later.

    Jean

MARIETTA

I looked around the room as she spoke, not out of disinterest, but in amazement. The back wall was sandstone, water dripped down it, tiny pockets of algae clung to the moisture. At the base of the wall, a trough collected the water where it then trickled off into a metal spillway on the outside of the building.

"Would you mind doing the onions while I shuck the oysters?" she asked. "I guess we'll call it a chowder. Or a stew. Oyster stew. It's good to have some company for a change. I've been eating as many of the oysters as I can, but it is getting a little boring."

I started to peel the crisp outer layer off an onion, trying to remember if cutting from the root first or last prevented crying. She'd put three large onions on the table and climbed on a chair to look in one of the top cupboards. I spoke above the noise of pots and pans clanging.

"I don't think we quite got around to introducing ourselves. I'm Claudine."

She was back down beside me chipping some burnt bits off an aluminum pot with her fingernail.

"You're right, we didn't. My name is Marietta. It's up to you what you make of your time here. I won't pry, but please feel free to tell me, or ask me, anything."

She sat down heavily in a rocking chair. The motion seemed to catch her off-guard until she relaxed into it. I lit the stove and poured some oil into the pot to sauté the onions.

"There's canned milk, flour, and pepper on that shelf just to your right. Get that going then I'll toss the oysters in," she said. "You must be hungry if you came over the mountain. I'm almost afraid to ask what the power station looked like."

"There were wires down, pylons were down, and some kind of building was smoldering. In the middle of the lake there was a fountain of water shooting about fifteen feet in the air. On the other side it looked like the side of the cavern had blown out. There's a waterfall. It's strange. It's salt water."

"I was hoping it was just a break in the aqueduct. This is terrible news."

The rest of the night absorbed into the strange flickering of electric and candle light. The conversation moved on its own, without a sense of purpose. The room was saturated in a purple glow, and throbbed with a contentment that sometimes follows a good meal in a relaxed atmosphere. The things I had been questioning, the essence of my searching, seemed to be acknowledged here at the end of a journey, by a person I barely knew. But once engaging with her, I felt we had been destined to meet for this very purpose; an evaluation of my insight and what it was that had brought me to a virtual standstill in my life—except for the activity of examining it. Whatever I spoke about seemed relevant, connected to the present, important to Marietta. I felt so comfortable revealing myself that I didn't question her interest in me.

When a direction is taken it starts justifying itself, beginning by imposing a dismissal on all that's unexplored. Direction becomes a window in the semi-dark of night. We are peering in or we are gazing out? We will send you there in the resin box. In the undertow we will understand you have to go. I'll see you there against the grain of the resin box. On the narrow shelf, I'll see you there and I'll be asking, "Will you be my guide?"

I'll see you there one day, you're on your way in the resin box you made. I'll see you there, you're on your way and I'm still asking, "Do you believe in testing everything?"

The question to be answered is shaving off in splinters, honing the skill, severing the bone. But I understand the need. Without a weightless grey. I can't believe in heaven, but I can. I can't believe in heaven, but I understand the need—sometimes I believe they're the same. Asking, "Can you make a chisel from the bone?"

Thrown to the wave, thrown to the sky, honing the skill, severing the bone. Sound. Vibrant shadows without a weightless grey, asking, "Will you be my guide?"

In the beautiful home with a flat roof holding it down, pressing down, the occupants arranged themselves in geometric forms. One was taller than the others—the father. One was sicker than the others—the mother. The boy tried to get away. The girl was young and under their thumb. The mother got sicker and sicker as the father loosened his tie and stayed out with the boys, eventually driving their little car across the bridge very drunk. He came to the house, the beautiful house, and opened the door of the room of the one who was under his thumb and sat down in the chair and told the little girl the stories that he needed to tell someone, but not his wife and not his friends and not his son. He turned to the one under his thumb. And the little girl sat up in bed and rubbed her eyes and listened to her father, her idol, her father. She didn't know he was drunk, just sloppy and smelling of cigarettes and old booze. They didn't want her to go. Who'd pick up the pieces, who'd put them together? She tried to get away and they looked at her as a traitor, a geometric outcast. She tried to get away and her mother told her that's how she got sick—from the one who was under her thumb. She told the girl she was not a pretty girl and that the boys only wanted one thing. Only one thing from the girl who was used to being under a thumb. They would try anything to get her to stay in a beautiful house with a flat roof pressing down, holding them down. Don't open the door. No one comes in, no one goes out from within. And the mother got sicker and the boy ran away and the girl stayed forever—under their thumb.

Where do I go when it's time to tell the truth? Where do I go when I need to rely on myself? Where do I go to cast the second stone and who is handing it to me? Where do I go to answer for myself and who is asking it of me? Where do I go to stand in line? I cast the first stone over my shoulder—lucky as salt.

Following the river one way to the sea. Following the river blowing back to me. Sailing on that ocean in 1533, riding on a wave, pulling down. A stranger is breathing in the back of the night, in the back of the dark, in the back of the dark of the night. The hawk. Reaching up. Reaching up to me. Following the river draining out to sea, following the river back to me.

"Are you going to tell yourself that long story again?" Marietta asked. "You know you hate the end."

I stared at her, finding her eyes in the dark. She was still rocking methodically, hypnotically. I was confused. I'd never met her, but she was claiming to know my story, to have heard me repeat this story to the point of asking whether I needed to tell it again.

"I hope you'll find a way to tell me what this story is

supposed to mean to you. The story goes—tell me if I'm wrong—you tried to walk to Tower Island, the island carpeted with shards of love. You never made it, you got halfway out into the river and the current pulled you under," she said without any hesitation.

The story, as she told it, didn't sound like anything I'd ever said, but something about it felt familiar. She'd delivered it with such confidence that I couldn't separate conviction from influence. Maybe that was her point. Maybe we all have stories of a journey to Tower Island, maybe we'll never get the details exactly right. Who shot Elvis? Who drowned the Kennedys? Who climbed Mount Rushmore? Who swam the seven seas? The gate was closed before the race was through. My movements made me look worried. She didn't have to look to see. I didn't want to know anything so well. I didn't want to give up so easily.

"No one wants to see you skidding across oyster shells in the back of the shucking yard, Claudine," she said quietly, encouraging me. "Come on, Pink Pearl, no one wants to see you reclining anymore, asking favours with your outstretched hands, stroking your green ring finger. At least not today. Why don't you lie down at the feet of the monster? Peach-A-Vanilla, lie down and unwind the gauze from your own wounds. Claudine, you control all your plans, you never meant to be lucky that way, but somehow you ended up on the fighting side. There's no reason you shouldn't trust yourself, but you find it hard just the same. All you have to look for is the strength in yourself. Who can tell where it begins and ends? I'm in it now and I can tell you, it doesn't end."

I awoke the next morning to the smell of smoke. I was in an upstairs bedroom under a heavy quilt. I got up and looked out into the courtyard. Marietta was fanning the fire under a cast-iron bathtub. The rusty metal chimney leaked smoke at the elbow. The tub was behind a screen of sweet peas that obscured it at ground level, but from where I was, upstairs, I could see the water heating up, bubbles forming across the bottom of the chipped white porcelain. I pulled my head in the window, shivered, and noticed the smell of coffee. I followed the smell downstairs to the kitchen, which I saw for the first time in daylight. Candle wax had dribbled across the table. Two calico cats were on the table, lapping at the remains of the oyster stew on our plates. The coffee was on the stove in a blackened espresso pot. I poured it and added canned milk that had gone a bit crusty and yellow around its little triangular opening. I was examining the herb garden on the windowsill when I heard Marietta call, "Claudine! The fire's started up again! I'm being boiled alive!"

I chuckled and called back, "Coming!"

When I got there I put out the embers with a ladle of water from a wooden bucket. Marietta laughed and squirmed in the tub to avoid the hot spots. I'd brought my coffee out with me and in a hazy half-awake state I started to think about the night before. I tried to separate dream from what was not. Marietta and I seemed like old friends now. I sat on a little water logged stool near the tub and breathed in the combination of sweet peas, sea air, smoke, strong coffee, and soap.

"Would you mind giving my back a bit of a scrub?" she asked, looking at me over her broad shoulder. I put down my cup, picked up a bristle brush from the table of bath things, rubbed soap across it and started to tell Marietta about finding my cabin.

"I pulled the brambles off the doorway, yanked on the

handle and the whole door came off its rotten frame. I found a lantern inside and I lit it. That felt like an encouraging sign."

I scrubbed Marietta's freckled back, watching the soap pull over her in streaks.

"I decided to stay overnight. That first morning in the woods was so peaceful. I snapped out of the dark mood I'd been in. I hadn't felt satisfied for a long time. I'd invented my own work, my whole life, but I couldn't seem to live in the moment, I couldn't seem to enjoy what I accomplished along the way. I had a great job—I illustrated cookbooks. I would go down to the test kitchen and the chef, the editor, and I would plan a menu. We didn't do the duckling in orange sauce the same day as the lamb shoulder with fresh mint! We'd make a soup or salad, a main course, and a dessert. While the chef was doing his final check of ingredients and proofreading the recipes I'd do the illustrations in fairly loose water-colour. I love food and I love painting—it was great. But the editor started to want more—*je ne sais quoi*—more changes, was what it amounted to. It started to become a grind."

Marietta settled back into the tub, basking in the morning sun.

"He wanted the grapes a little larger. Or maybe I could change the colour of the oranges to make them grapefruits in the fruit bowl. Water-colour isn't the best medium for altering things like that—it starts to lose its freshness and that's what I was good at. It was disappointing that he didn't value that aspect of it. Once he wanted me to add a chihuahua he'd borrowed from a pet store to give the tamale recipe a more Mexican feel. He'd have brought in the Eiffel Tower for the paté de la maison if it had fit through the door. There were never any conclusions to the projects that I could savour. Even eating the fabulous meals started to feel like the result of some kind of failure. Apprehension turned quickly to dread, and I became more and more unhappy. I wasn't having much success at adapting to the editor's new attitude and it started affecting me negatively. That's what was going on when I found the cabin. When I woke up that first morning the trees were flickering green, the wind was slapping branches against the roof. I just lay there and listened. Even though it was damp and musty in there I felt a kind of peace I hadn't felt in a long time. I normally carry a sketchbook with me on hikes, but I was drawing less and less. That day, when I walked outside, I took it out spontaneously and drew wildly, filling page after page. It was a strong reaction. I was euphoric. Before I knew it, it was dark again. I stayed another night and started planning my return."

"Listen," Marietta said. "I'm going to get out of the bath now, could you put another pot of coffee on?"

"Sure. I guess I've been going on about myself a while now."

"That's fine, really," she said. "It sounds like you need to talk about it."

"I guess I do, although it is strange to be telling you all this. I hardly know you."

"That's what this place is for. And that's why you've found me here," Marietta called after me as I headed for the kitchen.

I put the coffee on and thought about our conversation. Marietta came into the kitchen in a robe. She tossed her hair back and unfolded a towel with a big green dinosaur on it.

"Let me try to explain something to you about being here. It's a place to come and look at yourself. Whether you come here intentionally with your preconceptions, or you get here by accident, like you did, it's still the same place. You will learn something vital about yourself by being here, something you'll be able to draw upon in the future. This is not what it's supposed to be—a false light on the faces we can see. They're not really smiling, they're frozen into shapes. Translate them and you'll see they're power mixed with pain. No astronomer can pilot across a vacant night sky, a solid thing travelling with a blinding hole. Sometimes this light is called winning and I really don't know why. This light contributes nothing, it only allows you to see a false machine in motion passing through the clouds. It's not supposed to be. The false light we're afraid to name, passing through the clouds. These ghosts are normally seen in pairs. I'm an exception. Our passion to live evaporated. What choice do we have but to endure eternity superimposed on what we like to think of as reality? We're not involved in a dialogue devoted to success or failure. I get the impression from the letters people send back to their ghosts that they expect stories from some place called beyond. People write letters asking for information on potential fates. And then there are the ones who understand the spirits. I should take you down to the shed where all the letters are stored. I've tried to keep them neatly filed. You're welcome to have a look at them, maybe that will give you a better idea of where you are. And of where you're not," Marietta laughed.

After coffee we went back outside and started walking to the beach. We headed for a shed with a corrugated metal roof. Inside, shelves were filled with letters. It was overwhelming. I went back outside and sat on the steps of the shed with a bundle of envelopes postmarked 1910. Some of them were addressed to Marietta. Seagrass whipped across my legs, making them itchy. It was hard to imagine ghosts in the middle of a sunny day. It was hard to imagine Marietta being a ghost.

Ghost. Guest. Host. Complexity is the ghost of understanding. I tried to bring back the overwhelming sense of certainty that I'd felt when I was on the cliff approaching the waterfall, but I couldn't recreate that calm. It had only lasted a few minutes, but at the time, it seemed to clarify everything without complication. The world and everything in it seemed ultimately and obviously at peace, as if there were no unconnected components to be dealt with. The euphoric part of this sensation—and it was a sensation rather than a thought—was that there was no other way for things to be and that they had always been this way and would always be this way. I wondered how that information could produce the sensation it did, but that seemed to lead me to the type of thinking that was in opposition to the conclusion I'd drawn. I was trapped trying to decipher the words on the wall. A ghost. What is a ghost? What's left after life, a life that ended without peace, someone, something to be feared. A ghost is unpredictable except for its dissatisfaction. Phantoms between the mortal and immortal world. Complexity. Made up of related parts. Repressed feelings which cause abnormal mental states. Preoccupation. Complexus. A network of nerves or vessels.

Understanding. Not intelligence but tolerance. Complexity. Not difficulty but multiplicity. Ghost. Not to be feared, but what lingers on after history has had its say.

ALL YOU NEED IS A PEN AND PAPER

M*arietta,*
Hi. It's Tuesday. The door is open and it's raining. Very grey. Cars go by and their tires swish. Yesterday I went down to the courthouse for my first appearance. I was not on the list of accused or charged. I was sent upstairs to the registry to ask why. I was in the stairwell, between floors, and I had a strong urge to run away from this whole thing, but I didn't. The registry wasn't open yet so I went across the street to the lawyers' office. They weren't open either but I rang the doorbell and a fairly young guy with an earring and jeans let me in. I didn't know if he was the janitor or what. It turned out that he was a lawyer and really easy to talk to. He recommended that I go back and sort it out with the registry. When they opened, the clerk called up my case on the computer and said there was nothing there. That's probably the first time I've had a good feeling about a computer! I was sent downstairs to check in with "charge approval." Going to get my charge approved also seemed like a good thing to run away from, but I went in and found that my file had been returned to the police who will decide whether or not they want to proceed with charges! Ray says people dream of this happening. So they seem to have found a reason why this whole thing might not be worth bringing to trial.

As for money—I'm not totally sweating it yet. I'm trying to find a balance between hustling up cash and not wasting time that I should be putting into the book. Between money trouble and starting the week with a court appearance my mood swims around: pride, humiliation, defensiveness, gloom, self-pity, anxiety.

I had a good talk with an editor on the phone. He put together

131

a plot summary for the book. I had submitted one to my publisher, but he said it was "arcane." I had to look up "arcane." I guess I'm writing another book that's trying to defy being "about" something. What is life "about"? I guess it's a mystery of sorts. A mystery to me! The editor I spoke with was great—he got me to talk about the book and he kept typing, trying out different ways of saying things, revising and reading it back to me. I'm just now at the point where I have to wrap the thing up. Having someone else create a blurb-sized nugget was helpful even though at this point I haven't really fulfilled the outline—I prefer to leave things ambiguous, open to interpretation. I feel like I'm breaking the rules, but maybe that's not the worst thing. Language feels like it can be the greatest liberator and the greatest inhibitor. It gives you the most freedom, all you need is a pen and paper, but it has big limitations. I've been writing the book in chunks and then shuffling them together—it's amazing how they fit. It reminds me of running a film—like a home movie—and you put on some music; there are so many points where the sound and image just seem to connect. In fact, it's difficult to get a completely unconnected sense between image and sound. I believe the brain does some of the linking up—I don't know if that's the result of too much TV, but it seems like our brains try to convince us that things are in sync.

What I have written here will be some of the final pages of the book. Every few minutes my eyes leap up to the clock and I think I must stop this letter and get back to work on the book. Then I remember: this is the book!

One other thing, the publisher wants to change the name from "Complexity Is The Ghost Of Understanding" to "The Ghost Of Understanding." I wonder what you think of that.

I hope you're well. Thanks for your encouragement and support. It means a lot to me. I'm including the plot summary and I'll send the book when it's finished.

Plot Summary

After being charged with manslaughter, Claudine retreats to a solitary life on a wooded peninsula. Always on the razor's edge between "order" and "chaos," Claudine re-examines her sexual encounters beyond the realm of rigid feminist analysis. She discovers a derelict system of aqueducts and tries to find their source.

"Are we always drawing backwards?" she asks the mirror in her cabin. Her explorations lead her to a satori-like revelation and solves the mystery of the aqueducts. Continuing down the other side of the mountain, she stumbles upon a shed filled with thousands of letters. These letters are correspondence with an enclave of spirits from the past, present, and future. Claudine's ultimate conversations with these ghosts urge her towards a more hopeful perspective.

Bye for now,
Claudine

IN CANADA

Hi, Ray. I'm just about to leave here, is there anything you want me to pick up on the way?"

"No, I've got everything."

"Dave wants to know what we're having for dinner, but I told him it's a surprise. How's it going anyway?"

"Pretty good. It was a bit smoky in here for a while, but I think we've got that cleared out pretty good now."

"Good—well, just open the door and a window. Did the smoke alarm go off?"

"No, not yet."

"OK. Do you think I should pick up some beer?"

"Well, I could go halfers on a six-pack."

"OK, I'll stop at Avanti's and get some then I'll be right up."

"So in about ten minutes?" Ray asks.

"Ray, you walk this route at least twice a day. You know it takes about twenty minutes and I still have to get the beer."

"OK, I'll see you when you get here and dinner will be really, really ready."

"See you soon!"

Living in a trailer across the road from the cows, you were supposed to milk before dawn. You don't get home in time and besides, you're ripped and torn. You're walked to the edge of the land and told, "Never darken this doorway again."

Kind of a killer, when you cross the world's longest

covered bridge on your father's bike to see your girl . . . with another man. She gets away to tell you, "You have a lot of pigeon shit on you."

That's what happens in the longest covered bridge in the world. Kind of a killer, when you drink a half a quart of whiskey with your bacon and your eggs every morning. You're bound to take a dive for a stainless steel sink and someone will have to decide at what point in flight, mid or otherwise, you died. And for that the first utterance is, "It's about time!"

Something a little sad when you walk the fifteen miles to your baby while your baby has her daddy's car. Things went missing, things got replaced, and a few people struck down the law of the land with only a butter knife in hand. In Canada.

It feels good to be outside after spending another day typing my book into the computer. It's Thanksgiving Day, Canadian Thanksgiving. I walk home thinking about crops harvested, fish caught, the beginning of dark and quiet months ahead. I get the beer, walk along Commercial Drive, and head up the hill with a stream of crows flying above me. I get to where I can see our place. The sliding glass door is open. I smile. I can't see Ray, but there is a warm yellow light inside.

Ray is at the stove when I come in. There are three candles, a huge bowl of cranberry sauce, and raw baby carrots. Ray is lifting lids and peaking into steaming pans.

"Wow, it smells great in here. How's it going?"

"Fine, we're almost ready."

"OK—just give me a second to get my coat off and wash up," I say as I'm trying to get near the stove to see what we're having. "Can I take a peak?"

"Sure," he says and pulls off the lid to reveal a cookbook

classic, picture perfect, breaded chicken surrounded by simmering mushrooms, which he later tells me are in a red wine and teriyaki sauce.

"Wow," I say with the enthusiasm I'd planned regardless of what anything looked or tasted like. Except that this really does look and smell amazing.

We sit down to eat. Also on the menu: Ray's famous potato skins filled with mushroom, onion, and Gouda, baked in the oven. There is almost nothing else to talk about except how good everything is. I make a little toast about how lucky we are to be surrounded by so many good things.

"Ray, I need one more sex scene for my book," I say between mouthfuls. "You've gotta help me with it."

"Claudine, you've got a good imagination, I'm sure you'll come up with something."

After dinner I open my backpack and start going through notes for my book. I've been carrying around some scraps of paper from the library that I'd planned to work into the book. I remember the day I wrote them down, I felt like some mysterious world was opening up to me. That was last winter. It was cold.

> volcanism
> continental drift
> reservoir linings
> water hammer
> analysis of surge
> yard gate
> slope protection
> stone veneer
> sediment transport
> hydrothermal vent

bridge failures
hot springs
"Ice Cores And Common Sense"
drill core analysis
single barrel conduits
construction of underground channels in Rome
the evidence of Frontinus
water commissioner of Rome
dust storms on glaciers
socio-economic geography and erosion
circulation on earth
water shed mapping
geothermal steam power
deep sea hot springs and cold seeps

I found the bibliography I'd compiled around the same time:
From Atlantis To The Sphinx, Colin Wilson. Virgin, 1996.
Complexity, M. Mitchell Waldrop. Simon & Shuster, 1992.
History of Hydrology, Asit K. Biswas. North-Holland, 1970.
Tape Op, Lawrence Crane (Ed.), 1996.

Ray says, "Hey, I almost forgot to tell you. Your sample stars arrived today."

I ordered them last week by phone from a 1-800 number in *Tape Op* magazine. I roll them out like marbles, kiss my burnt fingers, and get to work on starting my galaxy.

JEAN SMITH is a singer, songwriter, artist, and author. She formed Mecca Normal (with David Lester) in 1986, a band praised for its "radical reappraisal of punk rock" (*The Stranger*, November 20, 1997). Also a member of Two Foot Flame, her strong sense of feminism and social politics informs all her work, and in part influenced the Riot Grrrl movement of the early nineties.

Her first novel, *I Can Hear Me Fine*, was published by Get to the Point in 1993 and is available through Arsenal Pulp Press.

She lives in Vancouver.

"Ambiguity is as powerful as slamming your fist on the table."

—JEAN SMITH

DISCOGRAPHY
¿Who Shot Elvis? (Matador, 1997)
The Eagle and the Poodle (Matador, 1996)
Sitting on Snaps (Matador, 1995)
Flood Plain (K, 1993)
Jarred Up (K, 1993)
Dovetail (K, 1992)
Water Cuts My Hands (Matador, 1991)
Calico Kills the Cat (K, 1988)
Mecca Normal (Smarten Up, 1986)